W9-ACT-414

Stand-in for Murder

Stand-in for Murder

Lynn Bradley

ASBURY PARK PUBLIC LIBRARY
ASBURY PARK, NEW JERSEY

Walker and Company
New York

Copyright © 1994 by Lynn Bradley

All rights reserved. No part of this book may be reproduced or transmitted in any form or by any means, electronic or mechanical, including photocopying, recording, or by any information storage and retrieval system, without permission in writing from the Publisher.

All the characters and events portrayed in this work are fictitious.

First published in the United States of America in 1994
by Walker Publishing Company, Inc.

Published simultaneously in Canada by Thomas Allen & Son
Canada, Limited, Markham, Ontario

Library of Congress Cataloging-in-Publication Data
Bradley, Lynn.
Stand-in for murder / Lynn Bradley.
p. cm.
ISBN 0-8027-3189-9
I. Title.
PS3552.R2277S7 1994
813'.54—dc20 94-1239
CIP

Printed in the United States of America
2 4 6 8 10 9 7 5 3 1

This one's for
Bob, Family, Guida, and MG

Stand-in for Murder

▽

1

COLE JANUARY KNEW he should have stayed in bed the minute he swung his legs over the side and dropped his warm feet on her breasts. They were icy cold. Her pale blond hair was spread out in feathered curls on one side of her head, but the other side, the left side, was dark with dried blood and mashed against her skull. She had on a powder-blue teddy. One strap was twisted off her shoulder, the other missing. Her mouth was open, and so were her eyes—the brown one and the blue one.

He leaned over the edge of the bed and stared into them. "Contacts," he muttered. "Nobody's honest anymore."

Cole rolled across the bed and jumped to his feet. The air conditioner had chilled the tile in the bathroom to the same temperature as the body. He shuddered and splashed water on his face. Whoever she was, she was definitely in his apartment. And definitely dead. Linda had said one day he would be in more trouble than he could get out of, and this just might be that day. He hated it when Linda was right about anything.

When she left two years ago, taking Kevin with her, she had said he'd never make it as a private eye. So far, at least, she was wrong about that. He had risen from the rank of citation server and skip-tracer to that of Houston's top insurance fraud investigator. He'd also found a few runaways. He wasn't exactly rolling in bucks, and he was still driving the Chevy Luv pickup, but things were looking up—until he woke up.

He rubbed the blond hair on each side of his bald head into place. His light-gray eyes weren't nearly as bloodshot as they felt. He shook his head at his image over the sink. It was the last time he'd celebrate his birthday in the middle of the week. "Is thirty-six over the hill?" he asked his reflection. He didn't know, but it felt like it.

As he came out of the bathroom and reached for the telephone to call Homicide, the bedroom door banged open.

"Freeze!"

Cole froze. Then a smile spread across his golden stubble. He knew the officer couldn't see the other side of the bed from the doorway in spite of the size of the woman's breasts. He was glad he'd never moved the bed to the east wall like Linda had wanted. "Good morning, Fraizer. Where's Rose?"

Roy Fraizer holstered his pistol. "Jesus, Cole, I knew you lived in this project, but I couldn't remember your apartment number. I must've heard Dispatch wrong. Sorry." He leaned out the doorway and shouted down the stairs. "Cool it, Rose. Wrong address."

When he turned back to Cole, he shrugged. "You should've heard us knocking before we kicked in your door."

"I've got the loudest flush in the building. What's the deal?"

"We got a tip on a homicide at this address. I guess Dispatch took it down wrong."

Cole nodded. "Those things happen."

"You go on back to bed. I hear that was some party last night. Sorry I couldn't make it." He turned toward the doorway and flung the words over his shoulder. "Happy birthday, anyway. I'll just let myself out."

There wasn't anything Cole wanted less than the hassles the next few hours were going to entail. "Before you go, I want to show you something."

Fraizer looked him up and down and raised an eyebrow. "Doesn't look to me like there's any more of you for me to see."

Cole flipped a pair of jeans from the chair and jerked them on. "Over here."

As they rounded the end of the bed, Cole heard Fraizer draw in his breath. "Son of a mother frog! That's Molly Jones-Heitkamp! You've really gone too far this time, January."

"You don't think I had anything to do with her being here, do you?"

Fraizer looked at the slightly raised window beside the bed and scratched his head. "You saying she crawled through that window and bashed in her head?"

"No! I don't even know who Molly Jones-Whatever is, for the love of Pete. How do I know how she got in here? Or why?" Cole could feel his blood pressure rising. He jogged regularly and ate twigs and berries, but a situation like this would make the Statue of Liberty's blood pressure go up.

He had to think fast, and the twinge of hangover made his brain feel like molasses. He took a deep breath. "What say I'm not here. You find me at my office. One hour. I gotta pick up something for my son. He's coming down for a couple of weeks." If he talked fast, maybe Fraizer wouldn't keep up.

Cole scooped the cotton T-shirt off the floor and pulled it on. The Dinosaur Dash logo grinned out at Fraizer.

"Now, that's cute," Fraizer said.

Cole didn't care what Fraizer thought about the shirt. "Think Kevin will like it? I got him one, too."

He knew Fraizer was going to come back with something he considered important by the way he raised his toes off the carpet and rocked back on his heels. Cole didn't give him a chance. "I'll go straight to my office as soon as I wash my truck. What say? An hour?"

Fraizer's toes bounced down. "Wash your truck? Wash your truck!" He took a step toward Cole and pushed a large forefinger in his face. "Coleman January, if you think you got anything to wash off that truck that I ought to know about, you better tell me now, Mother Frog."

"Easy, Big Boy. Somebody puked down the right door last night." Cole ducked under Fraizer's arm and grabbed his keys and wallet from the dresser. "My office. One hour."

Fraizer followed him down the stairs. "You and I know you didn't do it, but don't you do anything stupid. You keep your mouth shut. I don't want Harris breathing down my neck."

Cole wondered how anyone could breathe down Sergeant Roy Fraizer's neck. His height had almost kept him off the force. Cole did admire his easygoing ways, and he often thought if he'd been Fraizer's size he'd have stayed out of a lot of trouble.

Sergeant Rose Johnson was waiting at the bottom of the stairs. She had helped herself to a bagel. She grinned up at him. "I knew this was your place, but I didn't let on. Thought you might be in trouble. Glad it wasn't you what got dead. I'd hate to lose a friend."

Cole had known Johnson almost as long as he'd known Fraizer, but he'd never thought of her as a friend. A competent cop. A gutsy gal. But friend? Maybe. At least they weren't arguing, yet. He didn't have time to argue. "I'm not dead, but my head wishes I was."

Without giving her time to ask any questions, he said, "See you in one hour. Promise." He dashed out the door, then spun around and shouted, "Feed Blondie!"

Cole didn't know if Mrs. Stewart had noticed anything during the night, but he did know from experience that if she had, she would also have license numbers and descriptions. From the day he turned in his briefcase as an insurance investigator for Texas American Life & Casualty, Mrs. Stewart had pumped him about his new career. She would have been an asset to any private investigator—a natural snoop, perfect for stakeouts. But being resident manager for the big apartment project pleased her mother. It was one of the status projects: landscaped, clean, and big enough for tenants to remain anonymous. Each two-story condo-style apartment had its own back entrance through a private patio. Most had shade at some time during the day from the crop of pine trees the builders had invaded.

As Cole walked into the front office, Jennifer Ann beamed at him. "Well? Surprised?"

Cole was always surprised by Jennifer Ann. She was all of nineteen and assistant–assistant manager. Whenever Mrs. Stewart went to Momma's and left her in charge, Cole suspected she tried to look twenty-five. She did. From her shoulder-padded red blouse to her shiny red high heels, she looked in charge of anything she wanted.

She wanted an answer from Cole, and he didn't understand the question. He stood there with his mouth half open.

Jennifer Ann batted her green eyes below the purple eye shadow and tapped her foot. "You know. The stereo. The delivery men brought it late last night from the midnight sale."

When his mouth started to close, she huffed. "I thought you'd be glad I let them take the key so they could set it up for you."

Cole's brain waded through the molasses and made a connection. He nodded slowly. "Sure. The stereo. Who did you give the key to, Jennifer Ann? Did you see what they were driving, Jennifer Ann?"

"Of course I didn't! They parked by *your* place. Don't you know where you bought it?"

"What did they look like?"

"I just saw the one that got the key. An average jock type, I guess. I don't go much for jocks. There's this guy at the bowling alley, see, and he—"

Cole wasn't interested in Jennifer Ann's love life, or lack thereof. "I want to tip them for being so prompt. How many men are we talking about?"

"I don't know. Like I said, I just saw the one that took the key. He brought it right back, too."

"Think. What color was his hair? His eyes?"

Jennifer Ann screwed up her lips like she couldn't decide whether to answer or cry. "I don't know. I . . . I don't think you're supposed to tip them."

She came around the desk, wringing her hands, and stood in front of him. "Please don't tell Mrs. Stewart if I messed up again."

Cole smiled. He wanted to shake the description out of her, but he smiled. "Let's just pretend I never bought a stereo. Nobody delivered anything." He took a deep breath and backed up a step. "No matter who asks. Think you can do that? I'll forget about the tip. I'll tell Mrs. Stewart you're doing a great job. Okay?"

Jennifer Ann nodded, then swiveled to a negative head shake. "No one delivered anything to your apartment last night."

"No matter who asks, unless I tell you different."

She nodded, her expression very serious, her eyes so wide Cole could hardly see the purple. "And you'll tell Mrs. Stewart I'm doing a great job."

"Check."

Jennifer Ann nearly knocked him off his size-eight shoes when she threw her arms around him and whooped. "Yes!" She backed up, straightening her short skirt. "If I keep this job six more months, I'll have enough to go to beauty college."

Cole rounded the 610 Loop into the Galleria area. Even with Houston's famous shopping area's chrome-to-chrome traffic, he still thought it was worth it to have his office there, halfway between his apartment in southwest Houston and downtown. The buildings around the Galleria usually made him feel he was in a sort of second Houston. The office skyscrapers, the hotels, the restaurants, gave off a rhythm and heartbeat. Excitement. Action. For once, he'd had all the excitement he wanted for a very long time—and it was going to be a very long time before it let up.

First, he had to find out exactly who or what Molly Jones-Heitkamp was; then he could decide what came next. He hadn't dared ask Fraizer. He'd have gotten a twenty-minute lecture on keeping up with city government or city crime, whichever the case.

When he entered his office, Henrietta was clacking away at the keyboard. Bless her, Cole thought. As far as he knew, she had never been late anywhere in her life.

Without turning from the screen or missing a stroke,

Henrietta Luna said, " 'Morning, Coleman. Sleep well? You missed your nine o'clock appointment. She was looking for her sister."

"Give it to Leslie when she comes in."

"She did and I did." She pulled a yellow stick-pad square from the front of her keyboard and handed it behind her.

Cole grabbed it on the way to his office. His dry cleaning was ready. He dropped the note in the trash basket. "We've got a little problem. Know who Molly Jones-Heitkamp is?"

Henrietta backed her wheelchair away from the computer and rolled in behind him. As he dropped into his desk chair, she did a wheelie and set her brake. With her hands wobbling between her waist and shoulders and her head bobbing in short jerks like a doll with a spring neck, she said, "Why, Mr. January!" She crackled, in tones reminiscent of Katharine Hepburn's in *On Golden Pond*. "It seems to me a boy of your age should keep abreast of the world."

"Dolly Parton!" Cole played their game, knowing she wouldn't let up if he didn't.

"Coleman! That's not humorous. I do a darn respectable Hepburn. And for your information, Miss Molly is twenty-seven, about five-five, possibly a natural blond, and the ex-girlfriend-slash-manager of Jimmy 'The Strangler' Strauss, the wrestler, whom she dropped to become the current companion of mayoral candidate Ruben Gomez." She took a deep breath. "They, meaning our Bayou City's society columnists, say she is this town's next leading lady."

"What color are her eyes?"

"Blue would be my guess. From the pictures in the newspapers, I'd say she takes after her father."

"Not anymore."

"Explain yourself, Coleman." She absently rocked the left wheel on her chair.

Cole left out the part about stepping on her body, but did tell her about the stereo delivery. When he thought he had covered everything, he shrugged and threw up his hands. "And that's about the size of it."

"Thirty-four D, you say?"

Cole grinned and glanced at his watch. "Fraizer should be here any minute, and I need a shower and shave. Did we hear anything from Kevin?"

"No, but I'll be here through lunch today. Leslie's due back from the courthouse, and she said she'd bring me a salad. Maybe we can find Sister before—"

The telephone cut her off. She knocked the brake free and whipped both wheels to grab the receiver off Cole's phone. "CJI Investigations."

She listened, then said, "Yes, ma'am. Hold, please." She pushed the hold button and held her hand over the receiver, too. "A real sniffler. I can hardly understand her."

Cole took the phone. A woman's distressed voice stammered, "Someone is . . . is trying to . . . kill me."

Cole said, "Now, now. What say we start with your name. Ms.—?"

"Molly Jones-Heitkamp."

▽

2

WHILE THE SHOWER rained on his slick head, Cole thought he heard Fraizer out in the office. He twisted the knobs and shut down the water.

Fraizer's stomping shook the building. "And what we have here is a failure to communicate! Get that contraption out of my way."

Cole could tell Henrietta didn't move. "He's not," she said, "going anywhere. You got a thing for men in the shower?"

Rose said, "I'll just wait out here, Roy."

Cole whipped the towel from the rack and smeared the fog from the mirror. Running his hand across his face, he decided this was not the time to hold out for a hot shave. Maybe Fraizer would let him get his Remington from the truck. He toweled off and splashed cologne in strategic spots. He wanted to smell good when he met the second Molly Jones-Heitkamp. From the address she'd given him, she was going to be a couple of notches above his usual client.

Henrietta yelled, "He's coming in!"

Fraizer filled the bedroom doorway, then stepped into the room and closed the door. He focused his vision somewhere past Cole's left ear and droned, "You have the right to remain silent. Anything you say—"

Cole stared at him. "That sounds like Miranda to me."

"—can and will be used—"

"Fraizer! It's me. Come on, Big Boy."

Fraizer's shoulders drooped. "For Christ's sake, Cole, get some clothes on."

Cole pulled a pink shirt from the drawer and a red tie from the rack beside the mirror. He held them under his chin. "This look good for my photo session?"

Fraizer said, "Nothing looks good for you right now, Cole. We're trying to locate Jack Heitkamp to get a positive ID on his daughter. You're our only suspect."

Cole shoved his fists through the starched shirt sleeves. "How 'bout those Astros?"

"I'm serious, Cole. I gotta book you."

As they walked toward Fraizer's unmarked car, Cole wondered if he would have a chance to meet the other Ms. Molly Jones-Heitkamp. If Jack Heitkamp thought that dead woman was his daughter, who had it been on the phone?

They circled to the back of the apartment complex, which housed only small offices and independent contractors. Cole suspected the conversion to offices was to maintain the declining property without having to repair it enough for living quarters. Nothing leaked or sagged, but it needed paint and landscaping. The landlord insisted that tenants use the back lot for parking and the front for customers. Although it was surrounded by an eight-foot chain-link fence, security was minimal, if it existed. Cole had never seen the gate closed.

The asphalt on the back lot was soggy from the heat. It felt like a sponge carpet. The sound of traffic on Post Oak Boulevard, behind them by three blocks, was a deep ocean-roar sort of throb. Or maybe a snoring beast, Cole thought. A beast that woke with nightmare siren-screams in the middle of the day or the middle of the night. A beast that watched humans struggle through life's game, hoping for a home run.

Cole needed more than a home run. His truck was parked near the gate. Fraizer's car was close to the building, about halfway down from the end where they turned between the two units of the complex. Cole wondered why Fraizer hadn't parked in front, but he was glad he hadn't.

As they turned toward Fraizer's car, Cole said, "Thanks for not using the cuffs."

The big man shrugged.

Rose said, "You got enough trouble without chapped wrists."

Cole pointed to his truck. "Mind if I get my razor? I hate to show up without a clean shave. You know how Harris is about neatness."

Fraizer looked at him and cocked his head to the side. "You're not thinking anything funny, are you?"

"Aw, Fraize, you know I wouldn't do anything to make you look bad. I just want to look good." Cole stuck his chin up toward Fraizer and scrubbed his whiskers.

Rose nodded. "Get your damn razor and let's get the hell out of Dodge."

"Thanks, Rose. I owe you one." Cole trotted to his truck.

"Two!" she yelled. "I fed your damn fish."

He hated to do it. He never had much respect for anyone who took advantage of a friendship. He knew he'd regret it later. But by then, maybe it wouldn't make any difference. Over his shoulder he called, "Be right there!"

Before either of the officers could answer, Cole scooted under the steering wheel and jammed the key into the ignition. The little Chevy Luv kicked up dust and spun out the gate.

Cole whipped the truck onto the street. Out of the corner of his eye he could see Fraizer and Johnson running toward their car. Rose galloped about as gracefully as a horse with a stone under its shoe. Fraizer, rocking from side to side like an overweight bear, wasn't more than three feet ahead of her.

By the time Cole reached the stop sign at the corner, he guessed they were pulling into the street.

It was a good twenty minutes to the westside Memorial area of Houston. Cole stretched it to thirty-five by zigzagging over to Westheimer and cutting north at the Sam Houston Toll Road. Somewhere along the way, he lost Fraizer and Johnson.

He thought his timing was about right. He didn't want to arrive without a shave or before Molly Jones-Heitkamp. She had said she was calling from a friend's house, but wanted him to meet her at her home just off Memorial Drive.

The houses in the subdivision were all over three thousand square feet; most were two-story. The tall pines and oaks that made the area so desirable to others made Cole feel hemmed in. He took the winding drive and alternately watched for the street sign and checked the rearview mirror for patrol cars.

The circle drive was just as Ms. Jones-Heitkamp had described it: steep and wide. To Cole, it looked big enough to accommodate a small cottage with room for a garden plot. White posts supported the upstairs balcony that put the front door in deep shadows.

Cole parked at the top of the drive and climbed the marble steps to the front door. He would have liked the beveled-glass pattern set in the oak door if he'd had time to admire it.

As he reached for the door chime, the door swung in. The half-step up the threshold didn't account for the height of the man in front of him. He was dressed in loose knit pants that ballooned out like a harem girl's, then were gathered in at the ankles. They were pink. Combined with jogging shoes the same color and a cranberry sash, they made it hard for Cole to take him seriously. Just before a laugh burst from him, Cole got a good look at the bronzed muscles rippling across the bare chest. He was certain that bronze shouldn't ripple. He guessed the man lifted low riders for warm-up. The mature giant of a body was topped by a boy's head, complete with lopsided grin and freckles the color of old pennies.

Cole kept both hands at his sides. "I have an appointment with Ms. Molly Jones-Heitkamp."

The grunt could have meant anything, but Cole took it to be affirmative and stepped toward the doorway.

The boy-giant bobbed his kinky carrot locks and stepped aside. "This way," he grunted.

Cole walked behind him, across the terrazzo entry and off to the right. Down two steps of mauve carpet, the room opened up to the full two stories. An interior balcony swept across the left wall; a white marble fireplace faced them. Spread out on a pale-green brocade sofa to their right was Molly Jones-Heitkamp.

After Fraizer's identification of the body, Cole expected her to be blond and probably to resemble the dead woman. He had not expected her to *be* the dead woman.

She raised herself up slowly and stretched. "You're early." She looked at her watch, a heavy gold chain with a ring of diamonds circling the face. "By three and a half minutes, Mr. January."

"I try to be prompt. Especially for a beautiful woman."

She did not smile. "I see you've met my bodyguard."

"We weren't formally introduced."

"Jon, bring our drinks out to the patio. What'll you have, Mr. January?"

"Ice water would be nice." Cole wasn't too swift, but he noticed she was much more collected and in charge of herself than when he had talked to her on the phone. Her voice was steady, almost detached. He had no trouble imagining her in a blue teddy.

Her white sundress hugged her full breasts and extended to a high collar that left her with completely bare back and shoulders. The full skirt was short. Very short, Cole noted. Her calves were developed like a tennis player's or runner's. Both her eyes were blue.

When they settled into the white iron furniture beside the pool, Cole calculated that Fraizer would show up any minute. He didn't have time for small talk. "Why do you think someone is trying to kill you? Where were you when you called?"

She smiled a slow, cool smile. "You do move fast, don't you, Mr. January?"

It looked as if she were going to be one of those clients who need the slower approach. For those, Cole believed the quickest way to get them to open up was to keep quiet—a variation on the old salesman's saw that the first one to talk loses.

He was still waiting for her to speak when Jon brought the drinks on a white plastic tray. Plastic was definitely out of place in all the opulence. After Jon returned to the house and closed the sliding glass door, Molly leaned forward. Her eyes were an intense, honest blue that drew Cole toward them like a huckster draws a crowd.

She whispered, "A bomb."

Cole wasn't sure he'd heard right. He'd been more than slightly distracted by her leaning forward. "A bomb?"

"Jon found it under my car this morning."

Cole wondered what Jon was doing under her car. Probably lifting it. "Do you have any idea who would want to kill you?"

She leaned back and toyed with the celery stick in her Bloody Mary. "I suspect it has something to do with Ruben. That's where I was when I called."

Cole silently blessed Henrietta. "The Ruben Gomez who's running for mayor. Right?"

"Yes, we're an . . . item. I'm his campaign manager and"—she brushed a stray hair from her cheek—"his financial manager. I knew it could be a dirty fight, but—"

"Why would anyone go after you, when for the same nickel they could eliminate him?"

Molly stood up and paced toward the pool and back. "I have a very high profile, Mr. January. My father is Jack Heitkamp. My mother was Esther P. Jones. Perhaps you've heard of them."

It would be difficult to spend a week in Houston and not hear of them. It was impossible to grow up in Houston and not know they had done a great deal for the city on the banks of Buffalo Bayou. Esther P. Jones had endowed a large portion of the medical center, several parks, and a few scholarships. Those were the good points. Her stormy marriage to contractor Jonathan David "Jack" Heitkamp made headlines for the gossip columns until it all ended with her death in the Mexico City earthquake. That explained Molly's double name, but not why her relationship with Gomez would be life-threatening.

Molly took a couple of steps toward him and stopped. "Without my backing, my connections, Ruben wouldn't have a chance, even with the women and Hispanics behind him. In politics, who stands on your side is as important as what platform you stand on. Sometimes more so."

Cole didn't exactly follow her reasoning. "Still, wouldn't it be easier to discredit Ruben? Or if murder is the objective, kill him—not you?"

"That would be blamed on the opposition. If I'm out of the way, especially if it looks like an accident, Ms. You-Know-Who will still look good."

Cole supposed she meant the incumbent, Rosemary Townsend. Mayor Townsend had run a clean campaign in the past, as far as Cole knew. It was the transit problem and the question of who got what in the city contract-letting that started the questions flying. She wasn't looking nearly as good as she had during her first two terms. Even Fraizer had commented on her shaky ground and how he planned to vote against her.

Thinking of Fraizer, Cole realized there would be an APB out on him if he didn't get to headquarters. "Ms. Jones-Heitkamp, could you give me a list of people you consider possibles? Anyone at all, even outside of politics, who would have something to gain by your death."

"Please," she said, "call me Molly. Yes, there are three, maybe four persons I believe capable of such tactics." She set her glass on the round table and smiled at him. "Shall we go to the library?"

For a smile like that, Cole would go almost anywhere. But the library? Then he realized just how far above his usual clientele she was—she meant a room right there in her house. He downed the rest of his ice water and followed her through the glass doors. He noticed Jon slipping out the side door from the kitchen to retrieve the glasses, but Cole's attention was on the woman in front of him.

She did that swishy little move when she walked that made the short white skirt flare to each side in rhythm with her steps. Pulling his thoughts above her neck, he asked, "Have you lived here long?"

She answered without looking back. "Three years."

As they entered the library, she ran her hand over the volumes in the near shelf. "Daddy built these shelves especially for me."

There were several things Cole could think of he would like to do especially for her. All he could say was, "Nice."

The library was loaded with antiques and collectibles, but missed the stuffiness Cole associated with old furniture and overpriced junk. An airy film fluttered over the windows, allowing the midmorning sun to dance across the Oriental rug. Each painting and sculpture had its own spotlight aimed from the track fixture that ran the perimeter of the ceiling. Cole wondered if Daddy selected the antiques and art and if Heitkamp or Jones money bought them.

Molly copied the names and addresses from the index file on the refinished rolltop desk and handed Cole the scented notepaper. "Before you go, Cole, I think I should tell you—" She bit her bottom lip, looked at the ceiling, then shook her head and smiled. "I'm a very busy lady. If you turn up anything, anything at all, leave a message on my machine. Jon will be with me unless I'm at Ruben's."

Cole wondered what she wasn't telling him, but he didn't want to push it just yet. For now, Harris was his priority. Still, he did need more than names. "Before I go, I'd appreciate a quick rundown on each of these folks."

Cole took the quickest route downtown. When he walked into the police station on Reisner Street he went straight to Lieutenant Harris's office. He tapped on the door.

Harris bellowed, "Come in!"

Cole opened the door a crack and stuck his head in. "Anyone looking for me?"

"January, where the hell have you been?"

▽

3

COLE OFTEN THOUGHT Lieutenant Harris looked as if he had been grossly overweight and suddenly dropped a couple of hundred pounds. He was still on the chubby side everywhere except his face. There, the excess skin hung like a short curtain below his jaw. His jowls fluttered when he shook his head and bobbed when he nodded. The only time the jowls didn't move was when he was mad. That's when the little muscle at his temple twitched.

The muscle was twitching.

Cole knew he wasn't going to get any points for neatness. He bowed slightly and smiled. "Good morning, Lieutenant. How's it going?"

Harris jumped to his feet and slammed a file on the desk. "Damn it, January, it's two o'clock in the afternoon. Don't you 'Good morning' me. Get your ass in here and close that door."

Cole pulled the door shut behind him and held up his hands. "I swear I didn't do it."

Harris nodded; his jowls bobbed. "Hell, January, we know you didn't do it. She was moved, and she'd been dead for at least eight hours. Weren't you still at the party then?"

"I took a sick friend home, but she may not remember."

Harris almost smiled. "Well, check it out. And don't leave town."

Cole hadn't realized how tense he was until he expelled the air he'd been holding. "What say I just get on with my business, Lieutenant, and get out of your way."

Harris leaned forward, one hand on the desk supporting

him. "Somebody is trying to make you look seriously bad, January." He lowered himself into the chair and shook his forefinger toward Cole. "Don't you go making this case your business."

Cole said, "Not a chance. We got a little gal looking for her sister. Came all the way from San Antone just to hire me. Sweet little thing, she is." He made a mental note to ask Leslie if she *was* a sweet little thing as he backed toward the door. "Got any idea who the dead woman is?"

Harris nodded and bobbed. "Looks like it's Jack Heitkamp's daughter Molly."

"Wow! Is that a positive ID?"

"No, but we're—" Harris jabbed a finger at Cole. "Stay out of it, January."

The pay phone at Benny's Burritos was out of order, but the chili and beans did their job. Cole believed his brain worked better with a belly full of chili. Not just any chili. Benny's chili.

Each bowl was filled with lumps of meat and beans so thick they almost made it a stew. The red chili peppers weren't finely ground like most chili. Every few bites, he got a sliver of whole chili that pulled sweat from his body and tears from his eyes. The flavor and the garlic aftertaste stayed with him for a few hours. With jalapeños and crackers on the side, the meal was almost an out-of-body experience.

It was his only exception to a healthy diet, and then only in emergencies. Since Benny's chili held the distinction of being relegated to medicinal, the calories, fat, and cholesterol didn't count.

By the time Cole got to the phone at the service station on the corner, it was a little after three. Henrietta answered on the second ring.

Cole said, "Anything I need to know?"

She purred, "I'm sorry, sir, Mr. January isn't available at this time. I'd be glad to take your number and have him call you at his earliest convenience."

Cole grinned. "I've already talked to Lieutenant Harris, Henrietta. What's up?"

"Yes, sir, I expect to hear from him later this afternoon."

"Okay, okay, so someone is there that I don't want to talk to. Hold it while I get something to write on." Cole pulled out his wallet and sifted through a variety of business cards until he found one with a blank back. "Ready."

"Yes, sir, Mr. Manly. 555-1048. I'll give him the message. Thank you for calling."

Cole said, "You're a genius, Ms. Luna."

He hung up and walked to his truck. The right door looked like the bottom of the Dumpster behind Benny's Burritos.

While Cole sat in the truck with the car wash machine spraying the Luv clean, he opened the glove compartment and pulled out Henrietta's code sheet. He ran his finger down the list.

Mr. Manly or Menefee equaled man or men in the office. One meant she would handle it until he returned. The next two numbers were the time, so he should call back at four. Eight was Leslie; call her at home.

When the water shut off and the green light came on, Cole pulled back around to the phone. Leslie's line was busy. She could keep phone lines busier than Jerry Lewis's telethon, and she was the only person he knew who refused to pay the extra few dollars to get call waiting. She said it was rude.

Cole took the Gessner Road exit off the Southwest Freeway and turned north. Sometimes he envied Leslie her three-bedroom house in the quiet neighborhood. As he pulled into her driveway, he realized someone had to mow the grass and trim the hedge. His envy turned to pity.

The doorbell chimed the last of four notes as the door opened. Leslie had one hand on her hip and the other on the doorknob. Her short blond hair was wet. So was her face. Sweat circles darkened her pale-blue T-shirt under the arms and across the midriff. She was the same height as Cole. He liked that.

The first time Leslie came to his office, she had looked

him nose-to-nose and said, "You're just my big. We'll work together real good."

She was Texas kicker to the core, and Cole, who had grown up in Houston, thought of himself as a city boy with an occasional lapse into kicker, compliments of his ranch-owning uncles. But Leslie grew up in Cedarbrake, Texas, just north of the road between San Antonio and nowhere.

That first day, Cole had taken her to lunch. With her eyes wide, she had watched the stream of traffic passing Benny's Burritos. She had asked, "Doesn't anybody ever work around here? Back home nobody's on the street during the day unless they're going to pick up the kids from school or buy groceries."

After over a year in the city, she was still awed by the number of people on the streets during the day. She'd been right about one thing, though. They worked together real good. Cole knew there was a lot of small town left in her, but she looked like a classy city woman in her tights and T-shirt.

Cole grinned like he'd caught her in a fib. "You look pretty healthy to me, considering how sick you were last night."

"I told you it was the shrimp that made me sick. After I got rid of it, I was fine. I'm glad you finally woke up, Old Man." She did a couple of shallow knee bends. "But you can't read, Cole. You were supposed to call, not show up."

"Your line was busy."

"You're hopeless." She left the door open and walked toward the hall. "Six more minutes. Come on back."

Cole closed the door behind him and followed her through the house. In the back bedroom—the torture chamber, Leslie called it—was a miniature gym.

A bright blue mat covered the center of the carpet. Leslie climbed on a stationary bicycle in the corner beside the only window. A Stairmaster and rowing machine filled one wall; dumbbells and a weight bench were on the other side of the room. From a shelf in the open closet KIKK twanged a Randy Travis number loud enough to be heard above the bicycle's grinding.

Cole pointed to the radio. "Mind if I turn it down?"

Leslie shook her head in time with her pedaling. "We need to talk."

"That's what Henrietta said. What do you know about what's going on at the office?"

"Nothing you don't. It's the case I'm working on. Missing woman. Brunette, average height, good body. Sister says their grandfather died and left them a trust. She didn't say how big." She shook her head sadly. "You won't believe how little the woman knows about her own sister. Of course, maybe I didn't ask the right questions."

Cole caught the edge in her voice. "I'm sorry the case got dumped on you. You've got enough with that medical insurance fraud case."

"I called in my report to the insurance company. That's who I was on the phone with. The bozo was on the golf course early this morning and shot an 81. He didn't do it one-handed, either. Henrietta already has the follow-up papers."

"So, what's the problem?"

Leslie stopped pedaling and mopped her face with the towel draped across the handlebars. "It's not just one problem. I've been at Public Records most of the morning. I finally got a Social Security match and an address, so I went by." She shrugged. "Nobody home."

Cole said, "So? Sounds normal; middle of a working day."

"Right. I figure the lady's gotta make a living. No big deal. Right?"

Cole nodded. "Did you contact her sister?"

She stepped off the bicycle and picked up the 10-K jug on the floor. "No, I didn't tell her sister, yet."

Cole sat on the rowing machine. "All you had to do was find her. Right?"

"Pay attention, Cole. I found an address. I didn't find her. I found a name to go with the Social Security number Darcy Hayes gave me. Janice Phillips. That's Darcy's sister's name. But when I got to the address, the landlady said Karren, that's with two

Rs, Janson lives there. She didn't come home last night, according to the landlady. And—get this—she has a cat."

He gripped the handles on the contraption and pulled. "Who? The landlady?"

"Karren has a cat. The landlady heard it yowling and took pity on it. She fed it and took in Karren's mail, mostly advertising."

Cole threw up his hands. "Maybe she spent the night with a boyfriend, and her mind was on other things."

"Not likely."

"How do you know that? It happens." He knew it didn't happen to Leslie.

"Well, according to the landlady"—Leslie took another drink from the bottle—"Karren has lived in her garage apartment almost two years and never missed coming home. On a few occasions, she did suspect a young man spent the night with her, however."

"Well, Ms. Dick Tracy, what now?"

"You tell me. But first—" she glanced at her watch, "I take a shower. We've gotta call Henrietta, too."

Cole grinned. "Need any help?"

She cocked her hip. "In your dreams. Use the phone in the kitchen." She spun on one heel and marched to the bathroom.

He stood for a minute, listening to the water running and her humming. He could imagine her face up to the shower spray, her . . . He put the brakes on his imagination and shook his head to clear the vision before he reached for the wall phone. So far, he had maintained a good business relationship and a good friendship. He didn't want to ruin either. He called the office.

Henrietta said, "Good timing. He just left."

"What say you give me a clue?"

"Clark Kent."

"A reporter? What did you tell him?"

"That you killed her in a jealous rage."

Cole laughed. "And then killed myself?"

"I said I hadn't seen you and didn't have any idea what he was talking about. He was hard to convince. Said he'd be back with a camera crew if I didn't cooperate. I was very convincing."

"Okay, so you get the Oscar for the month. Hold the fort, Pilgrim. We're coming in."

"You do a lousy John Wayne."

"Hey, that was Gary Cooper."

When he hung up, Leslie yelled from her bedroom. "We can take my car. I don't want to ride in that sissy truck again."

"You didn't think it was a sissy truck last night when you decorated it."

"Okay, so I can't take the reminder of last night's dinner. But it'll save gas."

It was a practical suggestion, but Cole didn't like it. The derogatory remark about his vehicle gave him the excuse he needed and made the decision easy. He didn't have to tell her he never liked riding with a woman driver, even a better-than-average woman driver like Leslie. He did feel a certain obligation to tell her about his morning. They weren't full partners, but one of the reasons their business relationship worked so well was that he kept all his cards on the table, knowing she did the same. If either of them needed help with a case, the other one already knew the basic facts.

She had already said she needed his help, and this time he needed her help, too.

He didn't want to start off with "Guess what I stepped on this morning?" He stood beside her and watched her lock the front door. He followed her to her car.

When she opened the car door, she said, "It's okay, Cole. You don't have to tell me about it. Henrietta told me. Must have been a real shocker, too. How's it going?"

Cole breathed a sigh of gratitude. He liked that about his women. They took care of all the picky details and saved him a lot of grief. Of course, he knew they'd be hotter than a hamburger on a grill if they found out he thought of them as *his* women. He smiled weakly. "Confusing, very confusing, but not too bad."

He took the scented notepaper from his shirt pocket. "I've got three names to check out. Maybe one of them will confess."

"Three names! You've really been working hard."

Cole's expression was as serious as he could make it under the obvious adoration. He admitted that due to his expert questioning, Molly had been very cooperative. He did not include information about what a knockout body the society wench had. "Shouldn't be too difficult to find the killer. Whoever it is got the wrong blond and is still trying."

Leslie's silver boot earrings kicked at her chin when she shook her head. "I've got a funny feeling about this one, Cole. I'd rather stick with my missing person. At least when I find her, I'll make somebody happy."

Cole shrugged and headed for his little sissy truck.

The traffic was all outbound, but Cole and Leslie were headed east. Most of the parking lot was empty when they pulled into it.

Henrietta was on the phone. She motioned them to keep quiet. "No, I don't know when Mr. January will be calling in." She winked up at them. "Yes, I'll let you know the minute I hear from him."

She hung up. "Coleman, you've really stirred up a hornet's nest and made some folks ver-r-ry nervous. That was Judith R. Barnes. She'll call back later. You can count on it. She's called three times already."

Cole swatted the air at imaginary hornets. "We'll get those hornets, it's the killer bees—or is it the nosy reporters?—I'm worried about. Got any ideas?"

Leslie said, "You know I'd rather stay out of this one, but you're going to be a jerk and make me talk to one of your suspects, aren't you?"

Cole felt as if she were a completely different woman than the one in the shower. "Since you put it that way, and I'm still the senior partner, yes."

She clenched her fists and flashed a pseudo-smile. "I'm free till around seven. I figure I need to check on a cat about then."

Cole handed Henrietta the notepaper. "Make a couple of copies of this." He turned back to Leslie. "What do you know about Judith Barnes?"

Leslie said, "Just that she's Rosemary Townsend's right hand. Don't you keep up with anything?"

Henrietta wheeled back to them with the copies. "If you don't know anything about Judith Barnes, why is she on this list?"

"I know who she is." He turned and sneered at Leslie. "Molly told me. I thought one of you might know something else."

Leslie said, "If I knew anything else, I wouldn't tell you."

Henrietta tooted the bicycle horn mounted on the side of her chair. "Chill out, as my nephew says. We've got work to do."

Sometimes Cole appreciated Henrietta more than others. He would just as soon she would butt out of this one. But in the interest of getting the job done, he let it drop.

Trying to look as if nothing hostile had taken place, he said, "Somewhere in the back of my head the name Judith R. Barnes rings a bell, but I don't think it's connected with city politics."

He handed Leslie one of the copies. "What say you dig up what you can on her? I'll take the Strangler, and Henrietta"—he dropped the other copy in her lap—"you take what's-his-name."

Henrietta looked at the list. "Aw, Coleman, that's dirty."

Cole looked totally innocent. "I thought you'd want a chance to go to the theater at my expense."

Leslie headed for her office, then stopped and turned, her eyebrows drawn together, her nose wrinkled. "Cole, would you mind at least telling me what am I digging for?"

▽

4

MID-TOWN GYM AND Training Club was squeezed between General Joe's Chinese restaurant and a Circle K convenience store five miles from midtown. Cole had been there several times, once only about a week ago, looking for a runaway. The boy had come home the next day.

Cole still thought the club's chrome-and-white bodybuilding machines, blue carpet, and red track seemed out of place in the run-down neighborhood strip center.

Wrestlers and weight lifters huffed against machines and each other, making the piped-in music sound as if it had an offbeat bass player. Most of the men in the gym were younger than Cole by ten years. He checked his image in the mirrored wall as he entered and smoothed down the hair on each side of his pate that stuck up like Julius Caesar's.

He had changed to running shorts at the office and carried his gym bag, a gray nylon case with the new worn off. The T-shirt he had on was tight enough to show it wasn't the first time he'd been around weights. He squared his shoulders and walked briskly toward the ebony man beside the ring.

Hacksaw was not a name, or a man, easily forgotten. Cole put out his hand. Hacksaw's grip was as strong as the man looked. Cole didn't wince or pull away, but he wanted to. He thought he heard one of his knuckles break. He smiled to keep from crying. "How are you, Hacksaw?"

"Hey, Bantam." Hacksaw chuckled deep in his flat belly. "What have you lost now?"

"Three pounds, last time I weighed," Cole said.

The grunts of the wrestlers on the mat sounded as if someone was getting hurt—bad. When Hacksaw blew his whistle, the men untangled, scooped up their towels from the ropes, and shook hands. Cole was sure neither of them had a grip to match Hacksaw's.

Hacksaw dropped an arm that weighed as much as one of Cole's legs across Cole's shoulders and aimed him toward the row of machines. "I'll just show you the new lat-builder we got in case you decide to get some muscles on that skinny arm. Then I'll get you a locker key."

"Whatever you say, Hacksaw." He wasn't going to argue with a guy who could make Arnold Schwarzenegger look like a sick puppy.

Stale sweat and growing mold spores smelled strong enough to taste, and the temperature wasn't much cooler than the 92 degrees outside. Cole could feel his T-shirt sticking to his back. He shifted the bag to his right hand and immediately wished he hadn't.

After complimenting the torture machine, Cole said, "Just thought I'd go through the paces with the big boys. Is Strauss here? Someone had pointed out the wrestler to him the last time he was in the gym, but all he remembered was *big*.

Hacksaw grinned a white slash across his black marble face and stepped behind the blue Formica counter. As he pulled out the key box, he selected one of the small keys. "Strauss the Strangler is now Strauss the Struggler. I checked him in for"—he wiggled two fingers of each hand in the air around his quote—" 'treatment.' "

Cole raised an eyebrow.

Hacksaw leaned toward him. "The man has a little problem with moose milk."

Cole said, "Booze, huh? Sorry to hear that. Been there long?"

Hacksaw closed his eyes while he calculated. "About nine hours. Why? You going in the promo biz? He needs all the help he can get since his promoter quit him."

Depending on Strauss's condition when he had called

Hacksaw, the trip to Misty Glen Psychiatric Hospital didn't mean he wasn't guilty. Even if he was, Cole knew there was no way he could question him. "Just checking out a lady's friends," he said. "Do you know his ex-girlfriend?"

"You mean Golly-Miss-Molly? Or the bimbo that dumped him last night?"

It sounded to Cole as if Jimmy wasn't too lucky with the ladies. Not being a fan of wrestling, Cole wasn't sure, but thought he remembered reading that Strauss had a problem with his temper as well. Something about a lawsuit pending over some destroyed hotel property and a limo with the windshield busted out. Jimmy hadn't liked the room service or the ride. A fella with a temper like that was capable of anything.

Cole took the locker key. "Did you ever hear him say anything about his breakup with Molly?"

"Jimmy only comes to me when he's in serious trouble. When it comes to his social life, he talks to the press more than he talks to me." Hacksaw pointed to a man upside down on an angle board, doing sit-ups with dumbbells across his shoulders. "Hoss might know something."

"He doesn't look too friendly."

"He didn't used to be. I've been trying to get him straightened out for years. Now he's under the mayor's wing in that Youth Help Alliance program."

"You mean that badass-turns-good stuff?"

"Yeah, he's quit the steroids, and he's teaching street kids to wrestle instead of stealing their skateboards. And hanging out here instead of at the Purple Panther."

"I'm happy for both of you." Cole walked to the locker room and tossed his bag into the locker. He pinned the key to his shorts. Next, he took his gym shoes from the bag and pulled off his street shoes, an old pair of sneakers that were fine for walking short distances but didn't have enough support for running. He slipped on the new gray Nikes and tied the laces on his right shoe. He liked the Nikes. They made him feel as if he could outrun the wind. They made him feel ten years younger. They made him feel like the athlete he never was.

High school had been the worst. Any male who couldn't play football was scorned. He'd played until his junior year, then quit. He alternated between being ashamed of himself for quitting and proud of himself for coming to his senses. Most of the time he didn't think of it at all, but every time he tied on his new shoes, he felt like he was back in the game.

Cole had just tied his left shoe when Hoss entered the locker room. Hoss was the Bonanza heir's size, but gave no sign of the friendliness his namesake routinely exhibited. Cole nodded and closed his locker.

When Cole walked toward the door leading back to the gym, Hoss blocked him. "You got some questions." It was a loud, flat statement.

After the squeeze from Hacksaw, Cole wasn't too interested in shaking hands with an experienced wrestler. Hoss looked like an experienced wrestler. Cole smiled and reluctantly put out his hand.

Hoss's wispy, light-brown hair was shoulder length, tied back with a rubber band. He had a twisted bandanna around the top of his head with a glitter pin shaped like the Lone Star State on the knot over his right eye. His weight belt was wet with sweat, and his muscles bulged above it like a big bouquet of flowers jammed into a small vase. He had small blue eyes, sunk back in his skull more from a slightly swollen mat burn across his forehead than from basic structure. Cole figured the pink raspberries on his knees indicated he spent time on them that was not in prayer. If he was off the steroids, it didn't show.

Hoss leaned back and folded his arms across his chest. "Jimmy and me go way back. What hurts him, hurts me. You got that?"

"I don't want to hurt anybody." Cole wondered what Hacksaw had told the man. "I hoped you could tell me what you know about Jimmy and Molly Jones-Heitkamp." He watched Hoss's eyes, but couldn't read anything. The man was completely expressionless. "If you don't mind," Cole added.

Hoss relaxed his arms and grinned. "Naw, I don't mind. I was just checking out my kick-ass routine for tomorrow's bout. I got this actor-friend that's coaching me."

"You made a believer out of me," Cole said.

"Hacksaw says you're a runner. We can talk on the track."

Cole chuckled. "I can run and talk for about three minutes. After that, I have to breathe." Actually, he could talk for the whole three miles, but he didn't want to sound too cocky. Especially in the Mid-Town Gym and Training Club.

In less than two laps, sweat was sliding off his head and washing into his eyes. If there were any disadvantages to being bald, no hair to hold the sweat out of his eyes had to be number one. With the air conditioner on the blink, he didn't know if he could make his full run. The talking didn't bother him; mostly he listened.

Hoss told him only slightly more than nothing, but took six laps to do it. He'd only met Molly a few times; always thought she was bad for Jimmy. Made him try to be something he wasn't. Society stuff. That was when Jimmy's drinking got out of hand again. When she cut him loose, he had complained about all the time he'd wasted with her.

Hoss stopped for a paper cup of Gatorade from the dispenser, then caught up with Cole. "Jimmy didn't let any turf grow under his tootsies before he had a new squeeze, either. But last night his new lady said adios, and it really tore him up."

Cole didn't comment.

Halfway around lap seven Hoss said, "Jimmy's okay. He just gets a little pissed off sometimes and doesn't know his own strength. He's gotten some bad press."

Cole figured he was referring to the hotel problem.

Hoss said, "He'll be better when he gets out of treatment. He always is—at least for a while."

Cole pulled up his shirttail and wiped his head, again. "That's good. Thanks, Hoss. You've been a big help."

Hoss jabbed him in the ribs. "Wuss. That's no three miles. Heat gettin' to you?"

Cole glanced up at him. "How old are you, Hoss?"

"Twenty-six."

"When you get to be my age, you'll be able to run three miles in half the distance, too."

Hoss was still scratching his head when Cole trotted toward the showers.

At first Cole thought he had passed out in the sauna, but he couldn't remember going in there. A mosquito buzzed past his ear. He knew there weren't any mosquitoes in Hacksaw's sauna. They had more sense.

Cole jerked his hand to slap at the persistent insect and hit the dashboard. His eyes popped open. The convenience store's red-and-yellow sign quivered above the windshield like a painting on black velvet. Cole twisted his feet from under the steering wheel and sat up.

The last thing he remembered was reaching for the truck door handle and thinking how bright the old red paint shone when it was clean. He rubbed his head, trying to clear his brain, and found the knot behind his left ear. Whoever clubbed him knew where to hit. But why? He hadn't found out anything that wasn't common knowledge, at least in wrestling circles.

The clock on the dashboard said eight, give or take a few minutes. It never had been accurate. Cole hadn't been out very long. There was a pay phone just outside the Circle K, but Cole thought it might be wiser not to stick around too close. If his attacker came back and went for the other ear, he wasn't sure he'd come to before morning.

Taking the shortest route to the office got him there in twenty minutes. He found the note Henrietta left. She was going to catch the performance at the theater and would talk to her assignment afterward. Leslie hadn't reported in as of seven, it said. It was almost eight-thirty, and there was still no message on the machine from Leslie.

If she didn't report in soon, especially after what happened to him at the gym, he'd have to start looking for her. It wasn't like her not to let Henrietta know where she was. That was one of the reasons they used the machine instead of a live answering service. The machine recorded intonation, mood, and exact message, not unlike Henrietta Luna.

In theory, Cole and Leslie were supposed to routinely check in whenever they were on a hairy case or away from the office for long stretches. Cole had the even hours, Leslie had the odd.

As Cole pushed the button to roll the phones to the machine, the second line lit up. He aborted the transfer and clicked into line two.

Sergeant Rose Johnson said, "Cole, you owe me. That's dinner, at least, but I'll settle for Astros tickets."

Cole said, "I'd rather owe you than beat you out of it, Rose. What say we do Jack-in-the-Box tomorrow night?"

"Double or nothing, and I'll tell you what I know."

"Is this for sit-down dinner or cafeteria?"

The smile left Rose's voice. "You decide. They finally reached Jack Heitkamp. He's on his way in from Chicago."

Cole rubbed the lump behind his ear. "So?" He knew the victim wasn't Heitkamp's daughter. What did Rose expect him to do?

She shouted into the receiver. "Cole! He'll kill you!"

"Calm down, Rose. Nobody's going to kill me." Sometimes Rose could get an idea in her head that didn't make sense to anyone but her. "I didn't kill anyone. Harris said that's already been established."

Rose huffed. "Jack Heitkamp won't care what's been established. That girl's body was found in your apartment." She mumbled what was probably a string of curses, ending with, "I don't know why I care what happens to a jerk PI like you. The world's overloaded with jerk PIs."

Cole laughed. "Admit it, you got a thing for jerk PIs."

Rose slammed the phone down before Cole could tell her he'd seen the real Molly. He paused, unable to forget Rose's concern. If she knew he'd been knocked out, she'd want him to carry his .38 Special. Working unarmed never bothered him when he served citations or looked for missing persons. He didn't know if it bothered him on this case or not. He knew carrying a weapon wouldn't have kept him from getting the knot on his head.

As Cole reached for the door to leave the office, he saw the full-page hand-lettered sign taped to the back of the door: "KEVIN ARRIVING FLT 103 NEXT SAT NOON."

He couldn't keep from grinning. He slapped the sign a high-five and bounced out the door.

When Cole pulled into his covered parking slot, his mind was still sorting through the information he'd collected. Nothing made any sense. Why hadn't he just told Fraizer and Johnson to go see Molly? At least that would get Heitkamp off his trail. Or would it? What if the woman he had met wasn't the real Molly? Or what if it was, and Jack meant to kill her? Someone wanted her dead. But if she was the real Molly, who was the dead woman, and why was she hauled to his apartment? His apartment. That was the real question. The answers weren't coming.

He lifted the small bomb Molly had given him from the floorboard. It seemed too light to be effective, but some of the new explosives didn't weigh much.

As he got out of the truck, he heard a car door slam. He hadn't heard anyone pull in behind him, but he guessed it was a neighbor. One of the reasons he liked his apartment complex was the security gate. No one came in without knowing a code. He reached for the gate handle to his back patio.

Suddenly, he heard someone running toward him. Without hesitating or thinking, he turned and ducked—and wished he were armed.

Leslie came to a halt in front of him. "Where the hell have you been?"

Cole slapped his forehead and ran his palm across the top

of his head and down to his neck, trying to calm himself before he spoke. "Don't ever do that again."

She hung her head and cuddled the towel in her arms. "Gosh, I'm sorry, Cole."

It might have been a shadow, but he thought he saw a tail. "Whatever you've got, it better not be a stray cat."

She smiled and held up one hand. "On my honor, it's not a stray."

"Good. I want to show you something."

She followed him into the apartment. "You show me yours, and I'll show you mine."

Cole slid the glass door shut behind them. "Did you talk to Judith Barnes?"

"She had to go out of town sort of sudden. Her secretary said something about a funeral. I'll catch her tomorrow when she gets back." She peeled back one corner of the towel. "Look at this."

It wasn't a stray. It was a cat. Karren's cat.

By morning, Cole didn't like his new roommate any more than he had on first sight. If she rubbed his leg one more time, he was going to kick her across the room. Not deliberately. Probably not at all. But he wanted to. He did not like cats in general, and this one especially. She had long fluffy gray hair, a kind of mashed-in face, and blue eyes that were spooky. He'd given her his last can of water-packed tuna, and Leslie had donated kitty litter and a litterbox for the duration. If she didn't find Karren—or Janice?—soon, she'd have a missing cat to find, too. That, or she could take the cat home and feed it to her dog.

Other than the cat, which Leslie called Fluffy and Cole called It, his apartment was almost back to normal. The police had taken down the yellow plastic ribbon. Cole had wiped up the fingerprint dust, but the chalk on the floor was still faintly visible in the carpet in spite of Hoover's best. Without thinking, Cole stepped around it. He picked up the phone and punched in his office number.

After Henrietta got in her complaint on the unfairness of having to sit through an amateur production of *Brighton Beach Memoirs*, she said, "Gerald Payne lived up to his name. A real pain in the derriere. I didn't get any straight answers from him. But then"—she altered her voice, and Cole knew she flicked an imaginary cigar—"I don't think he's straight, if you get my drift."

"If you get my drift?" Cole said. "Wasn't that Walter Brennan?"

Henrietta let out a sigh of disgust. "Close enough. Are you coming in?"

"No, I've gotta see a man about a mule. If you haven't heard from me by noon, send the posse." Cole put down the phone and scooped up It. He held her at arm's length and placed her in the bathroom with the litterbox. Leslie would pay for this.

Hacksaw tilted his chair back on two legs and studied the "bomb." "I never saw anything like it. No detonator. No explosive." He focused his gaze in the general direction of the window and concentrated before making his pronouncement. "I'd have to say it's like a stage prop. All show and no blow."

Cole extended his hands. "How's Jimmy?"

Hacksaw rocked forward and dropped the bomb into Cole's palms. "Won't hear anything till he gets out of detox. Then he'll start the calls." His laugh said the situation was more pitiful than funny. "Don't know why that boy can't get it through his head that he can't drink."

Cole stood up, still holding the bomb with both hands, though it easily fit in one. He wasn't going to risk shaking hands with Hacksaw again. "I guess alcoholism's a lot like walking pneumonia. If you don't think you've got it, why take the medicine?"

When Hacksaw opened the door of the small office, they stepped into the main room of the gym. The air conditioner was working; so was Hoss. Hoss nodded at them from the bench, his face red, his muscles bulging, but the weights over his head steady.

Cole waved, then turned back to Hacksaw. "Did you notice if anyone followed me out yesterday?"

Hacksaw shook his head. "I wasn't even up front when you left. I was going to tell you about the special we've got on Powersticks. You ought to try them. They'll keep you on your feet that last mile."

As Cole drove, he unwrapped the Powerstick. It didn't look like a bowl of Benny's chili, but he was hungry enough to eat shiny blue wrapper and all. He had checked in with Henrietta; all was quiet on the western front.

Cole wasn't on the western front. Channel 2's radar screen promised rain, but Cole never trusted weathermen, even when he should. A loud clap of thunder was followed by the big drops hitting his windshield. He wondered if the predicted flooding was on its way, too. The slap of his wipers applauded the dust and rain, but a nick in the left blade left a muddy arc on the windshield. Ducking to see under the streak, Cole cursed the little things that make life difficult—the little things that are so easy to overlook, until it's too late.

Traffic slowed to a crawl at the Loop. Cole took the off-ramp at Westheimer, then turned under the freeway and headed toward town. Even in a downpour, the show must go on, he reasoned.

All Citizens' Theater—ACT, as its aficionados called it—was a small equity theater off Kirby Drive that prided itself on bringing theater to the masses. Cole had seen a play there several years ago. Linda had insisted. The two-story building hadn't changed much; the paint was more faded, and a new blue-and-white awning kept the poster on the door dry. "Neil Simon" in boldly outlined letters danced across the top of the poster, just above "Brighton Beach Memoirs." The contemporary art was local and not bad.

Cole brushed the wetness off his head and patted the bomb in his pocket. The lobby area was vacant, the lights dim. The usual array of eight-by-ten glossies graced the wall. Stars, past and present, smiled down at him. No one he recognized. The desk against the far wall held neatly stacked programs. Cole plucked one off the corner stack and scanned it. Mr. Gerald Payne was playing the father of the lead. The fifteen-year-old star in the production of Simon's comedy was from California, with a list of credits that would impress only his mother.

Cole heard footsteps off to his right and turned. A smiling old woman, her shoulders square and her chest out like a soldier's, marched toward him. "Follow me," she ordered.

Cole dropped the program back on the desk. "I'd be glad to, ma'am, but I may not be who you think I am."

"Nobody ever is around here." She crooked her hand and motioned for him to hurry. "Just fix it."

Following the nimble woman across the lobby and through the concession area,. Cole caught up with her and gently held her upper arm. "Ma'am? I'm not here to fix anything."

Her eyes widened, and her hands slapped her cheeks. "Oh, how silly of me. Of course you're not." She gripped his hand and pumped it. "I'm Ruth Golden, head of wardrobe. My main machine is down, and I've got wardrobe repairs to make before curtain tonight."

Cole opened his mouth to speak, but Ruth stopped him. "Whatever you're selling, I don't have time to hear about it." She whirled around and, much faster than her wrinkles indicated she could, dashed up the stairs.

When she was about halfway up, a male voice called down to her. "Can he fix it, Ruthie?"

Cole slammed his foot on the bottom step. "Just a minute, Ms. Golden. I want to ask you a few questions."

She turned and shooed him with both hands as if she expected him to fly away like a frightened pigeon. The man behind her, at the top of the stairs, came down two at a time and stopped in front of her. "I'll take care of him, Ruthie," he said in a stage whisper that was likely heard across the street.

Ruthie traipsed back to her busted machine.

Payne pointed one of his long tapered fingers at Cole. "See here, my good man, we're busy. You'd best be on your way."

Cole pushed to depict a note of awe. "Gerald Payne?"

Payne's expression changed from formidable to friendly so quickly Cole thought he had read him wrong. Payne gracefully swept his right hand across his torso, then extended it as he bowed. "If it's an autograph you're seeking, I'll be most accommodating." He smiled like royalty toward a repulsive but necessary subject.

As Cole climbed the few steps between them, the creak of the wood beneath his feet was the only sound. He slid his hand into his pocket and flourished the bomb beneath Payne's nose, then lowered it. "Ever see this before, Mr. Payne?"

Cole thought he saw a hint of recognition before Payne tipped his nose toward the ceiling. "Never!"

Cole said, "I saw in the program that you played the Colonel in *Glory's Rising*. Wasn't there a small bomb in that one?"

"Of course." He wagged a tapered finger crosswise. "But nothing like that, I assure you."

Cole stepped toward the wall to go around him. "Mind if I ask Ms. Golden?"

Payne stabbed his hand against the plaster and blocked him. "That would hardly be worth your time—or hers. She was not with the troupe when *Glory* was performed."

Cole pushed past his arm and shrugged. "All the same, I prefer to hear it from—"

Ms. Golden came toward him with an off-white length of fabric draped over one arm and a pair of long-bladed scissors in the opposite hand. "Can't you see I'm busy?" She glanced at the bomb. "Go sell your gizmo somewhere else."

Cole dropped his head and took a deep breath as he raised it. "I am Cole January. CJI Investigations. There's been a murder, and—"

Payne sucked in a lungful of air and expelled it in a rush

of words. "Where . . . Wha—? Oh, Mr. January, we're so sorry. Of course we'll cooperate."

Ms. Golden's head nodded slowly, her gaze fixed somewhere near Cole's nose. "Mrs. Windslow—she's the director—will be right back. You probably need to talk to her."

Payne looked as if he had descended to the lowly ranks of nonactors for the first time. All his affected mannerisms disappeared. "Can I get you a cup of coffee or a soda, Mr. January?"

Cole's mouth had that healthy aftertaste that comes with too many vitamins per bite, and his rain-spotted clothes were uncomfortably cool in the air-conditioned theater. "Coffee would be nice. Black."

Without a word, Ms. Golden ushered him back to the lobby and indicated one of the worn tweed-covered chairs. When he was seated, she leaned down and whispered, "Don't be too tough on the coffee, Mr. January. I made it at eight-thirty this morning. I don't make another pot till Mrs. Windslow gets back from lunch." She winked at him and quickly departed.

The coffee was hot and bitter. The Powerstick flavor was scalded off his tongue. He wished it were back.

The woman advancing toward him beamed capped teeth and sagging facelift. Her hair should have been as gray as Ms. Golden's, but was flaming orange. Towering above Cole, she focused a steady, if somewhat watery-eyed, gaze on him. Her deep, trained voice came from her diaphragm. "What's this nonsense about a murder, Mr. January?"

Without waiting for an answer, she took three long strides toward the stairs and bellowed in the general direction of the second floor. "Ruth! Fresh coffee!"

Her lightweight turquoise jacket flared away from her large hips as she spun around and faced Cole. "Well? Speak up, Mr. January."

Cole slowly got to his feet. "You're Ms. Windslow?"

"Mrs. Windslow. I was married for forty-two years to the finest man to walk the boards, God rest his soul."

Cole pulled the bomb from his pocket. "Have you ever seen this?"

Mrs. Windslow slipped on the reading glasses dangling from the chain around her neck and silently examined the bomb. "It's been painted." She lowered the glasses and let them fall against her bosom. "Yes, Mr. January, we made it for *Glory's Rising*. Last March."

"Exactly who made it?"

"A young man, I don't remember his name. He was only with us one season."

"An actor?"

"No, no. A stagehand. Handyman." She waved her bangled arm. "They pass through here all the time. Looking for work. Hoping for a break. Seldom do they know beans about the theater."

"Could you describe him?"

Her face masked over as if granite had replaced flesh. "Please excuse me, Mr. January. I have a show to produce."

Cole followed her to the stairs. "You didn't answer my question, Mrs. Windslow."

"And I don't intend to, Mr. January."

"I'll go to the police."

"I suggest you do that."

Cole stared up the stairwell and considered going after her, but decided it would be a waste of time. It was Gerald Payne's name that was on the list. Henrietta's questions hadn't produced any information on the actor that wasn't included in the bio in the program. It seemed curious to Cole that he had yet to ask who had been murdered.

Cole heard a board squeak behind him. Gerald Payne, minus makeup and costume, was coming toward him from the stage entrance under the stairs. In blue jeans and T-shirt, the actor looked as graceful as a ballerina.

Payne's smile carried the tolerance of an indulging parent excusing his brat. "She's always like this before a performance."

Something about Payne brought out the worst in Cole.

For no particular reason, he wanted to ram his fist down the man's throat. "What's your excuse?"

"Fear," Payne said.

His open admission took Cole by surprise, but it was no surprise to him that it wouldn't take much to make Payne run. "Why haven't you asked who was murdered?"

"I'm not sure I want to know." He leaned against the banister. "Murder is such an ugly word. Murder and death. If it's someone I love, I'll cry because they're gone. If it's someone I hate, I'll cry because they got off easy. If it's someone I don't know, I won't care." He shrugged. "Why should I ask?"

"Maybe because the intended victim named you as a suspect." Cole watched Payne for some reaction—a twitch, a tightened muscle, a bead of sweat. Nothing.

Payne said, "Then perhaps you should tell me the name of my accuser."

Cole said, "Where were you Wednesday night?"

"Here. Dress rehearsal."

"After that?"

Payne stiffened. "See here, Mr. January, I'm not inclined to answer your questions any more than your secretary's until I—"

"How well do you know Molly Jones-Heitkamp?"

▽

5

IF EVER THERE was a perfect swoon, Gerald Payne pulled it off. His eyes rolled back, his hand flew to his forehead, and he gracefully slid to the floor. No loud thud. No shriek of disbelief. A glass-smooth landing. Slowly, completely, Payne landed on his back, arms flung wide. His eyelids fluttered slightly before they closed.

Cole leaned down and patted Payne's cheek. "Gerald? Gerald!"

He got no response from Mr. Gerald Payne. He walked up the first couple of stairs and knocked on the wall. "Mrs. Windslow! Ms. Golden!"

Ruth Golden poked her head around the corner. "We're very busy, Mr. March!"

"January!" Cole shouted. "Payne just fainted!"

Cole heard Mrs. Windslow stomping across the upper floor. She didn't slow up when she reached the stairs but stomped all the way down, hammering the carpet with her high heels.

"The very idea!" she boomed. "He knows perfectly well I won't put up with his vapors. They haven't been in vogue for decades. That twit would be more trouble than he's worth if he weren't such a good actor."

She didn't seem to be talking to Cole in particular; more to herself, he suspected. She mumbled her way to the puddle of Payne and planted a spike heel in his upturned palm.

Before she had brought much pressure to bear, he jerked his hand away and sat up.

Mrs. Windslow said, "What is it this time?"

"Someone's tried to do in Molly, and she's pointed a finger at me." He got to his feet and flung a hand toward Cole. "Tell her, Mr. January. Mr. Cold-from-ice-water-veins January."

Mrs. Windslow jabbed her hands on her hips and snorted. "Well?"

"He's got it right, Mrs. Windslow. I'm trying to find out where he was Wednesday night, and who made the bomb found under Molly's car the next morning. I'd really appreciate your help."

Just as Mrs. Windslow opened her mouth, an especially loud clap of thunder rattled the old building. She rolled her gaze toward the heavens and shouted, "All right! I'll talk."

When the sound faded she smoothed her dress, folded her hands, and bowed her head briefly. Then, looking straight ahead, she said, "Mr. January, I'll tell you who made the bomb. It wasn't a traveling handyman. It was my son. He was killed in an auto accident one hundred ninety-three days ago. Seeing it rather unnerved me." She glanced at him and smiled weakly.

Cole said, "I'm sorry, ma'am. Could I ask you just two questions?"

Payne said, "You don't have to answer anything, Marcia. Maybe we better call your attorney."

Mrs. Windslow pointed her finger at Payne's nose, almost touching it. "Hush, Jerry, or I'll tell your mother you were rude to our guest."

Payne ducked his head.

Mrs. Windslow nodded to Cole. "Ask your questions, Mr. January."

Cole said, "One, who had access to the props? And two, how late did rehearsal run Wednesday night?"

"Any of the cast or crew has access, and we quit a little before midnight." She straightened her spine. "Now, if you'll excuse me."

When she was out of hearing, Payne said, "I told you I was here." His smirk was as classic as his swoon.

Cole smiled slowly. "Ah, but you haven't told me how well or in what context you know Molly."

He sighed. "Oh, very well." He cleared his throat and paced gracefully in front of Cole. "As I am no threat to the ladies, which you no doubt surmised, I have escorted several to prominent affairs. Among them, one Molly Jones-Heitkamp. Our last outing was about two weeks ago. The Contemporary Arts Museum. The Newton Sculpture Exhibit. That sort of tripe is all there's ever been to our relationship."

Cole knew there had to be more or Molly would not have put him on the list. "You're leaving something out."

Payne shrugged. "I can't imagine what you could possibly mean. Unless, of course, you're referring to the little tiff we got into on the way back to my apartment."

"So you were in the car and no one heard you?"

"My heavens, no. I live near the museum. We were walking. I suppose anyone watching could tell we were having a disagreement. One would hardly consider it grounds for an extreme reaction."

"Payne, what say you quit dancing around the bush and tell it to me straight. If you can do that."

"Tacky, Mr. January. Tacky, tacky. But, as you wish."

Cole thought there was a slight chance he might uncover something. He watched Payne's eyes. Payne's stage training held fast, and Cole saw no more than the actor wanted him to see.

"She had parked in my driveway, which was about as close as one could get to the CAM that Sunday. I thought we were becoming friends. You know, more than escort and rich-bitch. My mistake."

Cole motioned toward the chairs in the lobby. Payne followed without interrupting his monologue. "I invited her up for a cappuccino and to watch the political debate on the telly. My companion was away, and I would have enjoyed her company. When she declined, I was disappointed, but understood. Though our political views are similar, I can't agree with her backing Gomez, and said so. He's a disgrace, the way he's gotten so conservative he'd have a redneck bully running the police department."

Cole nodded. "And that's when she got mad? Obviously just defending her candidate."

"No, no. It was after that. She made a crack about being seen coming out of my apartment. I laughed it off and made a joke of it, but it was crude and smarted a tad. But, I assure you—"

Cole helped him finish his thought. "But not enough to make you want to kill her." If Payne didn't quit rambling soon, Cole thought, he would have him picked up for talking without a license.

Payne jumped up from the chair and stared at Cole as if he were awed by the man's perception. "Exactly! Not anything to kill over."

"Are you sure that's all there was to it?"

Payne shrugged with upturned palms. "I was upset. Maybe I did say something about wishing she was dead, or hoping she got killed on the freeway before she got home. I probably stomped my foot, too. But that doesn't mean anything. Surely you know that."

"Thank you, Mr. Gerald Payne. You've cleared up a great deal. Tell the ladies good-bye for me." Cole wasn't convinced Payne was innocent, but he could only take so much of the man at one time.

Cole dashed from the building, hoping to keep his almost-dry clothes from getting any wetter. Instead of the big splashing drops that fell during the thunderstorm, the rain had settled in for a long-haul pattering of small drops squeezed out of the gray blanket overhead. Cole remembered his grandmother saying, "Big drops, over soon; little drops, all afternoon." He cursed the little things in life that never go away.

By the time he got to the office, Henrietta was well rehearsed. In the accent of "Star Trek" 's Scotty, she flipped the stapler open and talked into it. "Sorry, Capt'n, we'll never make Warp Five. The shields won't hold."

Cole grinned. "Does this mean the Klingons are about to board us?"

Henrietta set the stapler back on the desk. "It means the reporters won't give up. They want some answers the cops aren't giving out. You're a hot item to anyone who can pull off an exclusive."

Cole put a finger across his lips. "Hold that thought." He went to the dead-file cabinet, the only four-drawer upright file cabinet in the office. He had faced the press more than once, but usually over the phone. Most of his cases were small potatoes to the news media. Only the frauder and the fraudee cared. The media sometimes asked his opinion on whether or not a new law would affect the incidence of fraud cases, but he hadn't been a hot item since he caught a young man in a major, as in three-point-five-million-dollar, insurance fraud. Cole had lucked out. It was his first big case for Texas American Life, and the beginning of building his solo career. The arsonist, Tim or Tom something-or-other, had hung himself before the trial.

Cole slammed the top drawer and pulled out the next one. Running his finger across the tabs, he scowled, slammed that drawer, and pulled out the next one.

Henrietta quietly rolled up behind him.

Cole cut his eyes toward her, but knew she wouldn't speak until he did. She must have oiled that squeaky wheel, he thought.

He scanned the tabs, then threw up his hands. "Okay, I give up. Where'd you hide it?"

"Want to give me a clue, Sherlock?"

"Yes, Watson, that old file of clippings I carted over here when I left Texas American."

"Sorry, boss, that was before my time, and that file cabinet is out of my jurisdiction."

"You know, the one with all the newspaper clippings. It was in one of those big reddish-brown expandable files."

"Oh, you mean the Timothy Ross publicity clips? Bottom drawer. Ross, T."

"You're amazing."

Henrietta didn't blink or smile. "I know. Now tell me what to tell the reporters."

Cole pulled the thick file from the drawer and patted it. "I had some classic comments on this case. Look through here and see if anything applies."

Henrietta rolled back to her desk with the file on her lap. "I don't see how this could help. He was a suicide and you've got a murder on your hands, or under your feet, as the case may be."

Just as Cole settled into his desk chair, Leslie burst through the door. "Did Hot Shot Delivery get here yet?"

Henrietta shook her head.

Cole leaned forward so he could see Leslie from his office. She looked fantastic. Her hair was plastered to her scalp like she had just stepped out of the shower. Cole didn't even notice the makeup streaks down her cheeks. He watched her shrug out of her nylon windbreaker, shaking her breasts as she jiggled her arms out of the sleeves. His body realized where his thinking was taking him before his brain did. He jerked back against the chair and grabbed a file off his cluttered desk.

Leslie came into his office, drying her hair with a handful of paper towels. Her blouse was damp across the front. Cole could see the lace pattern of her bra. He scooted his chair up against the desk and tried to look casual.

Leslie said, "Cole, you are never in a jillion years gonna guess what I got for us for tonight."

Cole knew she wouldn't want to hear his first guess. "I give up. What say you just tell me."

"We are going to—are you ready for this? A fund-raiser barbecue at Judge Olsen's ranch!"

Cole groaned. "Aw, Les, do I have to? You know I'm not into politics."

She nodded gravely. "I got two tickets."

"What say you and Henrietta go?" He didn't think he should be alone with Leslie, considering the way he'd been feeling lately.

"No, sir. This is your case. Remember? I'm looking for a missing sister."

"What does this have to do with my case?"

"Judith told her secretary to get a pair of tickets to us."

Cole suspected he couldn't get out of going, but fired his last shot. "I have some errands to run. Need to pick up my dry cleaning. Gotta get ready for Kevin."

"Cole!" She stretched his name out to a full sentence. "You've got a whole week before Kevin gets here. I'll help you. Judith's secretary is having Judge Olsen's wife Hot Shot our tickets over here. I just left her office."

"Is Judith going to be there?"

Leslie nodded.

Cole moaned. "Oh, all right." Strictly business, he promised himself.

"How's Fluffy?"

Cole grinned. "There! You see? I gotta go feed It and Blondie. Can't make the barbecue. Pity."

"Pity, my hind end. I'm going home and change and you're picking me up at six-thirty."

They both turned at the sound of the door opening. The Hot Shot Delivery man handed Henrietta an envelope and got her signature on his clipboard form.

Cole said, "At least you know Barnes keeps her promises."

Leslie shook the rain off her jacket and draped it across her shoulders.

Henrietta said, "How're they going to have a barbecue in the rain?"

Leslie took the envelope. "A tent," she said. "A great big tent."

Cole followed Leslie to the door. "How formal is this shindig?"

Leslie flashed a satisfied grin. "Kicker all the way, so get out your best cowboy gear. That's how come I wanted to go in your truck, even if it is a sissy truck and darn near old as my daddy."

Cole did a rough calculation. Leslie was twenty-seven,

nine years younger than he. No way he was anywhere near as old as her father. Then he realized she was talking about his old Chevy Luv. He knew he'd better get a grip on reality. He'd never even noticed she was a girl until lately. He wasn't old enough to be her father, but he was too old to be thinking the way he'd been thinking about her.

While the committee in his head discussed his possible fate, he noticed that the freckles sprinkled across her nose looked like grains of brown sugar. He wondered if they tasted as sweet.

Leslie said, "Cole, did you hear me?"

"Sorry, I . . . I was wondering if Kevin still likes Mellow Crunch."

"I said don't be late."

About an hour north of Houston, they came to the Olsen ranch. The tall pine and magnolia trees obscured the house and outbuildings, but the entrance was well marked. The gate was decorated with sagging wet red, white, and blue paper streamers. Draped between two pine trees, a sparkling cloth banner proclaimed "Townsend Is Tops." Judge Olsen had thought of everything. Even the gravel road had been recently graded, but the rain had found the soft spots and washed holes in the roadbed. The red Luv bounced toward the ranch house behind a train of Suburbans, F-150s, and BMWs.

Cole was not looking forward to the evening. The cowboy directing traffic in the muddy field south of the house motioned for him to pull in behind the row of parked cars and drive to the far end of the field. Cole growled at Leslie. "You think they saved the back forty just for us?"

Leslie pointed to the couple riding the golf cart shuttle toward the house. "Isn't that the mayor? Who's that man with her?"

"All I know for sure is that it isn't Ruben Gomez. Maybe it's Jack Heitkamp. Didn't Henrietta say he was blond?"

"Oh, Cole, we better go home."

Cole swung the truck into a slot between a Suburban and a BMW. He wasn't in a running mood. Something about the boots and string tie he wore. Did it to him every time, he thought. From some faded Western movie he remembered, "There ain't no horse that can't be rode and there ain't no cowboy that can't be throwed." He didn't plan on getting throwed.

The rain wasn't more than a heavy mist, but by the time they reached the big tent they were more wet than dry. After Cole apologized to Leslie for not waiting in the truck for one of the shuttles to return, he promised to work his way to the bar and bring back a margarita for her. He didn't expect to see anyone he knew at any politically motivated gathering—especially this one.

He was next up at the bar when he felt the tap on his shoulder.

▽

6

"HEY, MOTHER FROG, whad're you doin' here?"

Cole whirled toward the sound. "Fraizer! Just the man I want to see."

Fraizer leaned toward him and whispered, "I never mish Olshen's blowout. Been friends since we was pups."

Fraizer's breath nearly took off the rest of Cole's hair. Cole said, "Maybe you better ease up on the moose milk."

Fraizer straightened up and grinned. "One beer for aroma and I can fool anybody. What can I do for you?"

"You fooled me all right, Fraize. I thought you were going to fall on me."

Fraizer cuffed Cole on the biceps. "I ought to fall on you, after the way you've treated me lately."

Cole faked a blow to Fraizer's midsection. "What can I say, Big Boy—I'm sorry?"

"Only if you are."

Cole stepped aside for two men leaving the bar with their hands full of frosty mugs of beer. "I'm truly sorry."

Fraizer patted Cole's bald head. "I know it, Mother Frog. Just don't do it again."

If it would keep Fraizer from messing with his head, Cole swore he'd never do it for ever and ever. He elbowed his way to the red, white, and blue bunting.

While he and Fraizer leaned against the bar and waited for their drinks, Cole said, "I had a little problem at Mid-Town Gym and Training Club. You know anything about the place?"

Fraizer winced and rubbed his left shoulder. "Sure do. Makes my shoulder hurt every time I think about it. A few years ago I went one-on-one with a big dude that called himself Hacksaw. Worst beating I ever took."

Cole held back a bubble of laughter that was working its way up his throat. Just imagining those two bears going at each other tickled him. He didn't imagine Fraizer would think it was so funny. He nodded. "That's the place. Hacksaw's the manager now. When I was leaving there, somebody whacked me on the head and tossed me in my truck. Got any ideas?"

Fraizer took a handful of peanuts from the dish on the bar and tossed a couple into his mouth. "Probably wasn't Hacksaw. You're walking. But somebody out there doesn't like you. I'll check it out. Unless you can give me a little help, I probably won't find anything."

"Later," Cole said, then switched to a country twang and drawled, "Tell me what-all I need to know to survive at this here hoedown."

"If you mean Harris, he's not happy about you giving me the slip. I don't care how sorry you are, you still owe me for that one, Mother Frog."

"Don't I always pay up?" He didn't wait for an answer. "So, what else do I need to know?"

They took the drinks from the bartender and turned toward the crowd. Fraizer said, "And if you mean Heitkamp, no problem. When he showed up at the morgue, he knew right away it wasn't his daughter. He's not sure somebody didn't mean to off her, though. The woman looked a lot like Molly, that's a fact."

They walked through the crowd toward Leslie, with Fraizer breaking trail. Fraizer turned and walked backward a couple of steps. "You ever meet Heitkamp?"

"Should I?"

Fraizer excused himself through the throng, holding his drink high above everyone's head. "He's a tough one. Not much for small talk. It's just a hunch, but"—he nodded hello to Leslie—"I think he's hiding something."

Leslie reached for the margarita and looked up at Fraizer. "Who's hiding what?"

Fraizer ran his tongue around his lips. "Food. It's in the next tent. Think I'll just mosey over there and see if they're ready to serve."

When Fraizer ambled off across the reception tent, Cole said, "He thinks Heitkamp is hiding something."

Leslie made a sound that passed for a comment, but wasn't. Cole hardly noticed. He was caught up in everything but Leslie. That was one of the things he liked about working with her. He didn't have to pretend to hang on to everything she said. They could be quiet without either one thinking the other was mad. It was never that way with Linda. She said he was moody and didn't know how to communicate. Cole liked being quiet with Leslie. A good working relationship, he called it. He planned to keep it that way—if he could.

He wondered what kind of relationship he would have with Jack Heitkamp. Fraizer said he had spotted Jack hobnobbing with the city council biggies. Cole couldn't decide if he should approach Heitkamp or wait for the man to come to him.

From where Cole stood near the front of the tent, he realized he couldn't see as easily as he could be seen. He took Leslie's elbow and guided her toward the center of the tent. "Don't you think we should thank our benefactor for this lovely opportunity to sweat with City Hall?"

Leslie drew a tissue from her handbag and blotted her forehead and upper lip. "I could have stayed home and worked out without making this much sweat."

"At least the rain finally stopped."

"But the humidity didn't."

Out of the corner of his eye, Cole caught the movement of a couple coming toward them. He turned toward them and noticed they acted as if they recognized an old friend.

The woman stuck out her hand. "Mr. January, I presume."

Leslie said, "Well, howdy, Miss Judith. This is a right nice party."

Judith R. Barnes, her chin-length dark hair swinging as she talked, pumped Cole's hand. She had the firm handshake of someone who's done a lot of handshaking. With her full lips and high forehead, she was a striking woman. She would never be called beautiful.

Probably a homely child, Cole thought. He said, "We want to thank you for the tickets, Ms. Barnes."

"My pleasure, I assure you, Mr. January." She waved her hand toward the man with her. "I don't believe you've met Jack Heitkamp."

He turned to face Heitkamp and was surprised to see him smiling. Cole couldn't decide if his smile was sardonic or satanic.

Jack Heitkamp was only a couple of inches taller than Cole, but Cole guessed his bulk was nearly double. His blond hair was military-short, and he had the sort of swagger that said he was used to walking in boots and giving orders.

Their eyes locked for a split second, then Heitkamp said, "So sorry for your misfortune, but relieved to discover my daughter alive and well. I understand you've spoken with her."

Cole hadn't expected that. Molly had insisted she didn't want her father to know she'd hired a private investigator. Had she also told him about the bomb? He sipped his Lone Star and slowly lowered the mug. "Yes, we've talked."

Heitkamp stepped back slightly. "She said you were verifying her existence. That you had to see for yourself that she is alive. Is that true?"

Cole pushed the Stetson to the back of his head with one finger, like the hero of an old Western. He smiled and nodded. "And she is very much alive, Mr. Heitkamp."

Jack Heitkamp's eyes relaxed. He smiled; then chuckled. "Indeed she is, Mr. January. Indeed she is." He slapped Cole's shoulder. "Call me Jack."

Cole said, "Frankly, Jack, I didn't expect to see you here. Aren't you supposed to be rooting for the other team?"

Jack stiffened. "I was on this team, as you call it, long before my daughter could even vote, much less muddy the water."

Leslie said, "Judith goes by Judith, not Judy."

Cole gave Leslie a sharp look. If she was trying to change the subject, this wasn't the time. He turned back to Heitkamp. "Just be careful not to let her muddy water splash on you."

Jack's expression didn't match the friendliness of his wink. "Molly and I have an understanding when it comes to politics."

Judith laughed nervously and brushed at an imaginary speck on her skirt. "Perhaps you two would like to be seated with us?"

The deep buzz of a loudspeaker quieted the crowd. From the far end of the tent, standing on a chair, Judge Olsen tapped the mike. "Is this thing on?"

A roar of "Yes!" came back to him.

"Okay, folks," Olsen said, "I don't want to interrupt your fun, but the barbecue you've all been waiting for is now being served in the dining tent. I want to thank our good mayor and—"

Cole didn't follow the rest of the introductions and thank-yous, but applauded along with everyone else. His mind was buzzing with questions louder than the microphone. If Molly didn't want Daddy Jack to know he had been there, how did the subject come up? If she lied about why he was there, did she lie about anything else? Why would Judith ask him to sit at the head table?

That privilege seemed a little excessive. Either Judith was overtly covering up guilt, or she was faced with a couple of cancellations at the head table. Leslie had pulled a few answers out of her in the ladies' room and whispered to him that Judith couldn't remember, but thought she was out of town the night of the murder. Did Judith understand she was being investigated for attempted murder and possibly murder, too? He still had a few questions to ask her, but talking while gnawing on spareribs was out of the line of duty. So much for a healthy diet, he thought.

When Olsen stepped down from the chair, everyone was pushed along by a wave of bodies. Cole and crew were funneled into the other tent like reluctant salmon being forced upstream. Cole was convinced Heitkamp didn't know about the bomb under Molly's car. If they had such a great understanding, why hadn't Molly told him?

The dining tent was set up with a long table across the far end for the mayor, city councilmen, and other notables. The other tables were just as long, but ran out from the head table in parallel rows. There were more than enough people to fill the tan aluminum folding chairs.

After the people went through the serving lines along the tent walls, they spread out to grab seats with friends or whomever they deemed to have the potential to grant favors or help them up the political ladder. Cole and Leslie followed Judith and Jack to the head table.

Leslie whispered, "I thought you didn't eat stuff like this."

Cole grinned. "Only in the line of duty."

Judith waved a hand and motioned for Cole and Leslie to sit at the left end of the table. Just as they sat down, a gaggle of reporters and photographers swarmed around them, firing cameras and questions.

"Where did you meet the Jane Doe found murdered in your bedroom?"

"What other cases are you working on?"

"Why aren't you under suspicion?"

"Is it true you were—"

Cole jumped to his feet with both arms raised. "Hold it!"

Everyone stopped moving; no one spoke. He faced the reporters. "What say you back off. I'll tell you this: You know as much, or more, than I do."

Leslie jumped up beside him. "He was with me."

Cameras clicked like castanets. Cole sat and pulled her down to her chair.

Judith stepped up beside the table. "I'm sure your editors will appreciate your efforts, but we are gathered here this evening to help our good mayor Rosemary Townsend raise support for her Save the Homeless campaign." She flipped her hair behind her right ear and smiled for the cameras. "Any contributions to the mayor's campaign will also be appreciated."

A ripple of disappointed comments filled the tent.

Judith said, "I know Mayor Townsend will be eager to answer your questions."

As the intruders lowered their cameras and tablets, Judith turned a tight smile toward Cole. "Cole, Jack has a few questions he would like to ask you. You don't mind, do you?" Her square jaw was set. Her eyes focused beyond him.

Cole held a sparerib halfway between the plate and his lips. Was that fear in her eyes? "I'd certainly like a chance to ask him a thing or two, myself." He nodded toward the dripping bone. "What say we have our little get-together after we eat?"

Judith guided his hand toward the plate. Cole released the food. She said, "This won't take long."

Must not have been fear of him, he reasoned. Ignoring his growling stomach, he followed her out the back of the tent.

Jack Heitkamp and a man almost as big as Roy Fraizer smiled as Cole approached the shadows beside the guy wire.

Jack said, "This is my foreman, James. He'll make sure you understand what I'm telling you."

Cole shrugged. "I don't have a problem with that, but James might." He suspected his smart mouth was about to get him into trouble again.

James looked at his boss, then at Cole. Cole smiled up at him. In for a penny, in for a pound, he thought.

Heitkamp said, "I'm very serious, Mr. January."

Cole said, "Hey, what happened to 'Cole'? Weren't we on a first-name basis?"

Jack jutted his jaw toward Cole. "You listen good, Mr. January. Stay away from my daughter."

For a big man, James moved fast. Cole was only slightly faster. He swung his arm down quick enough to take some of the power out of James's fist. The blow caught Cole just below his solar plexus and knocked the wind out of him. He doubled over, then brought both fists up together. Before Cole made contact with his target, another fist slammed into his jaw and rocked his head back farther than it could reasonably go. He stumbled backward, then regained his balance and lunged toward James. James grabbed him, jerked his arms, and twisted him around. He pinned Cole against his chest with his elbow crooked around Cole's neck. He squeezed.

Cole's anger was churning raw adrenaline, but no matter how hard he pushed against James, nothing moved.

Jack Heitkamp leaned toward Cole, his mouth just inches from Cole's face. "Just to make sure you understand, I repeat, stay away from my daughter!"

Cole squirmed under the headlock. James jerked it tighter.

Heitkamp said, "James will see that you get to your car."

The gumbo mud had seeped through his clothes when Cole finally came to. There were no new knots on his head. The nearest he could figure, James had squeezed until the lack of oxygen knocked him out, then dumped him on the ground beside his Luv.

Even though the last of the clouds had not disappeared with the rain, that didn't account for the total darkness. In the country, it was darker than he'd ever seen a midnight in the glare of city lights. Cole didn't think it was midnight. He hadn't been out long; the field was still packed with cars. The night noise of crickets, cicadas, and bullfrogs all sounded like strange birds to Cole. The only sound he could identify was the bass player holding the beat for the Western band. That throb from the tent guaranteed the party was far from over.

Cole sloshed toward the soft glow of the tent. After tripping and falling a few times, he slowed down and inched his way to the dining tent. At the back entrance, he motioned to the group of smokers collected there.

One of the men took a few steps toward him and turned back to the others. "Whoever he is, he's falling-down drunk."

All Cole wanted was for one of them to get Leslie from inside. He stomped to the tent. "I'm crazy, too! Get out of my way before I sic my wolf on you."

They did, as quickly as they could in the thick mud.

Cole stepped into the tent and scanned the faces staring at him. He couldn't find Leslie. He dashed toward the head table. It was empty. He jumped to see if he could spot Fraizer, but knew he'd left early.

Someone called his name. He turned in time to see Judith wildly approaching him.

"Cole! You look awful. I thought you got sick and went home?"

When he grabbed her by both shoulders, she jerked away and wiped at the mud on her dress. "What is the matter with you, Cole?"

He grabbed her again and held her. Her shocked expression reminded him of a surprised goldfish. "Who told you I got sick?"

She turned her nose up at his mudpack and groaned. "Jack said when he was talking to you outside, you said you weren't feeling well and wouldn't be coming back in for the dance. Leslie dashed out of here to drive you home. The poor girl hardly ate—"

Cole released her shoulders and dropped his angry gaze. "Sorry I got mud on you. Leslie didn't take me home, and you're telling me she's not here?"

Judith's eyes squinted down before they went wide. "Jack's gone!" She whipped her head from one side to the other. "No, no, Leslie's not here." She charged toward him, her chin just ahead of her tight fists. Her face was less than a foot from his when she spoke in a forced whisper. "You! You let them leave together!"

Cole backed toward the exit. No one was watching them, or everyone was watching them. It didn't matter. He had to get out of there—away from her distorted face and threatening fists. He'd never hit a woman and never wanted to. Judith Barnes was on the edge of changing all that.

The headlights behind him were on high and closing in. Cole swung the Luv to the far right of the four-lane highway to get away from the glare in his mirror. He'd gone to Huntsville, then headed south toward Houston, still slimy from his mud bath. At the first roadside park, he planned to pull over for a phone and rinse.

Bright-Lights was on his tail again. Cole started toward the inside lane, but the driver behind him stomped on the accelerator and shot up beside him. Cole eased up to allow the maniac to pass. He didn't. Instead, he cut the wheel and bounced the heavy Ford F-150 against the Luv.

The jolt caught Cole by surprise. The light Chevy truck scooted into the gravel at the side of the blacktop before Cole regained control and pulled it back onto the highway. Whether he sped up or slowed down, the Ford stayed with him. Cole quit trying to identify the driver in the dark cab and kept his eyes on the road.

There were very few cars on the dark stretch of highway, and those were coming from the south. Just beyond the reach of his headlights, Cole caught the small red glow of taillights with the row of amber lights high above that marked an eighteen-wheeler. If the lunatic beside him tried it again, Cole would have a witness.

He accelerated to shorten his distance from the cross-country trucker. Bright-Lights stayed with him.

Cole had never liked this particular stretch of road, and his current predicament wasn't making it any more likable. In the daytime, he especially disliked the way the tall pine trees and dogwood formed a wall between the road and the pastures. As dark as it was, Cole realized he couldn't see anything if the trees weren't there. Still, in more open country there would be lights from scattered houses to take away the loneliness and give him hope that he might stumble across some help.

At the moment, Cole wouldn't mind a little loneliness. The F-150 slammed against the Luv again. Loneliness sounded real good. Cole gripped the wheel and wondered if he'd die with his mud on. With the next blow the Luv bounced off the road, coming to a loud stop as it plowed sideways into three full-grown pines.

Cole killed the engine. The way it was hissing and coughing, he knew it wouldn't put up any resistance. Bright-Lights whizzed on down the road, leaving Cole to simmer in his gumbo.

The long walk to the nearest roadside park was close to five miles. To Cole's bruised body it felt like fifty, and took him over an hour. Midnight came and went before he dialed the pay phone.

"This better be good, Mother Frog. I don't like to have my beauty sleep interrupted."

"What say you just listen up."

While Cole waited for Fraizer he had time to think—and time to rinse off. He was physically beat, but his brain was boiling with anger and anxiety. Whoever rammed him knew where Leslie was. He was sure of it. He had to find her. Somehow he knew it was all tied to the murder, but nothing connected.

Cole guessed it would take Fraizer some time to start the process of checking on Heitkamp and running a make on James. Good old Fraize knew the right people. As soon as he got things rolling there, he'd drive all the way out to the rest stop and pick up the mother frog that jumped into the frying pan again.

Cole took off his squishy boots and crawled up on one of the cement picnic tables to conserve what energy he had left. His eyes closed, and visions of Benny's Burritos drifting across his mind, he could almost taste the steaming bowl of chili. Much better than the barbecue he didn't get to eat. As he nodded off, he mumbled, "Yeah, that's the ticket."

The sound of his own voice in the still, dark night jerked

him awake. He bolted upright. "Ticket!" he shouted. That was it! It was a setup. Judith gave Leslie the tickets to get him out there, so . . . so what? He wasn't sure, but he knew he could find out.

With that settled, he slid back down on the table and folded his arms under his head. Soon only the resident squirrels heard him snoring.

By the time Fraizer arrived, Cole was awake and almost dry. The stars were visible. The clouds had moved east and left a clear, sparkling black curtain overhead.

Cole didn't wait for Fraizer to stop. He jumped in the rolling sedan and grinned. "Never thought I'd be glad to see you."

Fraizer said, "You may not be when I tell you what I found out."

While Fraizer talked, Cole directed him to Leslie's house. As they pulled off the Southwest Freeway Fraizer said, "So, Heitkamp looks squeaky clean. We haven't found anything on an employee named James yet. The boys are working on it."

Cole said, "Jack's exact words were 'Stay away from my daughter.' Was it a father thing? Or was he afraid I'd find out something?"

Fraizer turned into the subdivision. "Fathers can be funny about their daughters, that's a fact."

Cole slammed his fist on the dashboard. "Damn it, Fraize, there's got to be something I'm missing."

"You could file a complaint, and I could bring him in."

"Where does Judith fit in? Or does she?"

"My best guess would be she doesn't, 'cause she's too close to the mayor. There's rumors that she'd do anybody in if it helped her, as long as it didn't make her look bad."

"There!" Cole pointed to Leslie's house.

The porch light was on, but the garage was empty. Cole rang the bell and stirred up Sandy. The dog set the neighborhood mongrels to howling, but nothing raised a response from inside the house.

Even though Cole hadn't expected to find her at home, he was disappointed and desperate. He turned to Fraizer.

"We've got to find her. Jack said he wanted to make sure I heard him loud and clear. You don't suppose he's kidnapped her? If he does anything to hurt her, I'll—"

Fraizer said, "We can put out an APB. Why don't I just take you home and get a unit on it?"

"What say you take me to get some dry clothes, and I go with you?"

His apartment smelled like a litterbox. Asleep on the counter that separated the living area and the kitchen, It was as close to Blondie's tank as she could get. Cole shooed her to the floor and dropped a few Tetra Floating Goldfish Pellets on the water.

There was nothing left to feed the cat but a can of corned beef hash, the last of his emergency rations. He opened the can and dumped the contents on a paper plate. Before he could set her meal on the floor beside the bowl of water It was on the counter again, going after the food like a starving infant.

In spite of himself, Cole chuckled. "Blondie, you're lucky I found something to feed this feline. If Leslie doesn't bring more food, you may be her next meal."

At the thought of Leslie he yanked off his boots and dashed up to his bedroom, shucking clothes as he ran. By the time he got to his bureau he was down to bare skin. He threw on clean jeans and a white dress shirt with a cuff button missing. He stuffed his damp wallet into his back pocket and reached for the nearest pair of shoes just as Fraizer barged in the front door.

Fraizer stood at the end of the stairs and yelled, "I got hold of the unit in Heitkamp's area. They're checking the place over."

Cole never functioned well on minimum sleep. He walked down the stairs and shook himself awake on his way to grab a bottle of raspberry sparkling water from the refrigerator. Then it hit him. "I just realized something," he said.

Brushing past Fraizer, he walked to the answering machine,

with its blinking red light, and jabbed the play-back button.

"Cole? Henrietta. Call me at home. Urgent."

Fraizer said, "What does your Nazi drill sergeant want at this hour?"

Cole didn't know, but he was going to find out. When Henrietta said it was urgent, it was.

The phone only rang once before Henrietta answered. She sounded half-asleep, but the other half was paying attention. Without formalities, she said, "Leslie called. Said for you to sit tight. She can handle it."

Cole groaned. "When did she call? Did she say where she was?"

He knew Leslie well enough to know she thought she could handle anything. She was almost right. Men like Heitkamp were an exception. They couldn't be handled. Not by a sweet country girl, no matter how tough she was.

Henrietta said, "She said she wanted me to know she was safe and would call you in the morning. I guessed she didn't leave a message on your phone. Something about getting home on her own." She paused. "Cole, what the hell's going on?"

Cole said, "If she calls back, find out where she is. And don't go to the door for anyone but Leslie or me."

"Coleman January, you answer me!"

Cole knew he'd have to dig himself out the next time he saw her, but he hung up anyway. Lately, everything he did got him in trouble with a friend. He grabbed the sparkling water and tossed a second bottle to Fraizer. "Let's go. Wherever Leslie is, there's trouble. We may have to save Heitkamp before this is over."

Fraizer gave a low whistle. "Sounds like your lady partner doesn't want your help."

He knew that. But what she wanted and what she needed weren't necessarily the same. Cole opened the front door. "You coming?"

"You got any ideas where we're going? I've got to report in before too much longer."

"Do you know where Heitkamp lives?"

* * *

Jack Heitkamp's house was surrounded by a six-foot white brick fence. Cole scanned the black iron spikes that decorated the top. Mounted in four towering pine trees, spotlights made the yard as bright as a Wal-Mart parking lot. He read the small red-and-white enameled sign on the gate. It said the gate could be opened with a card key or digital code. He had neither.

Cut through a large stand of pine, the winding drive made it impossible for him to see the house from the street. If there were any dogs standing guard, they weren't in sight, either.

Fraizer pushed the buzzer. "First we play by the rules."

They waited for only a few seconds before an electronic male voice clicked on. "There is no one available to receive you. Please leave a message and you will be contacted. If you persist, a security guard will be summoned."

Cole mashed the buzzer and held it down. "That ought to get someone's attention."

A spotlight flooded the gate area.

Fraizer leaned toward the microphone. "Police. Sorry to bother you, but we'd like to ask you a few questions."

Cole jerked Fraizer's shirt. "You trying to get us killed?" He ducked into the shadows in front of the brick fence.

After a short whirring sound, the floodlight blinked out, and the voice came back. "There is no one available to receive you. Please leave a message and you will be contacted. If you persist, a security guard will be summoned."

"It's a fake. There's no one there," said Cole.

"There doesn't have to be anyone there. We can't get through the gate."

"Hide and watch."

"Aw, Cole, you know I can't watch you trespass."

"Then close your eyes."

Fraizer turned and lumbered toward the car. "Come on, Mother Frog. Don't do it. You got any idea what Harris would do to me?"

Cole's voice was little more than a whisper. "Always thinking of yourself."

Fraizer glanced back. Cole wasn't there. He was perched on top of the fence, straddling the row of spikes as best he could. "Bye, Big Boy."

Cole dropped to the other side, praying the absence of dogs was permanent. He knew several tricks to throw a dog off, but none of them worked unless he planned ahead of time. The only trick he had in his bag now was the Nikes on his feet. Quietly, slowly, he worked his way toward the house.

▽

7

JACK HEITKAMP'S RAMBLING ranch-style house had once been featured in *Houston Town & Country* magazine as an example of gracious country living in the city. Cole could see why. The wide veranda was an inviting place to sit and whittle or rock a spell, sip lemonade or Lone Star. He figured the architect had never spent any time outdoors in Houston, Texas. If he had, he would know that mosquitoes take over verandas and everything else that's exposed as soon as the frost clears.

Cole stayed in the dense brush and pine trees that ringed the landscaped yard. As he groped through the dark perimeter toward the back of the house, he thought he heard voices. At first the sound was so muffled it could have been his imagination playing tricks on him. Or maybe a distant television blasting through the predawn quiet. The closer he got to the house, the more distinct the voices became. The deeper one was definitely Heitkamp. The other, also a man's, sounded almost familiar.

Cole dropped to his knees and stretched out on his belly. The grass was wet, but thick. He doubted if any mud could seep through. He'd had enough mud.

Scooting toward a small outbuilding and staying in its shadow, he got close enough to make out the silhouettes of the two men. They were standing between the main house with its spotlights and the driveway.

Between the men and Cole there was a swimming pool that at some time in the past must have been beautiful. Its graceful shape and Mexican tile coping indicated that no expense had been spared. Now it was empty. The cracked cement had shifted, pushed up by groundwater. Clumps of weeds had sprouted along the irregular seams.

The small building Cole approached was a prefab metal storeroom. Remnants of a water mattress were held by a prickly pear cluster at the corner of the shed. Cole skirted the thorns and dragged himself to the edge of the shadow. He was close enough to the men to follow their conversation.

Heitkamp said, "Don't come back here again. You know the rules."

"Yes, sir, Mr. Heitkamp. I'm sorry, sir."

Cole squeezed his eyes shut. He knew that voice. That body shape. From the gym? No, not the gym.

The man swung his arm and flipped the end of a sash around his waist. "You want me to take care of Miss Leslie?"

Molly's bodyguard. Cole was sure of it. A chill of fear washed over him. Then came the anger.

The next few moments etched vivid vignettes of motion and pain into his brain. He was running toward Jon. Jon turned, his leg outstretched. Jon's foot came toward his skull. Then stars. Lots of stars.

Cole was on his back, looking at the pale light just beginning to clear the treetops. Stars still studded the sky, but not like the ones he saw at first. The real stars were fading fast. Cole wanted everything to fade away as fast: the grinning redhead and smirking blond man, the problems, the fears. If only he had skipped his own birthday party, none of this would be happening.

Unless he moved, it appeared the scene wasn't going to change. He roared to his feet, shaking his head and dancing on his toes like a champion boxer.

Jon grinned. "Want some more, huh?"

From the shadows, Fraizer yelled, "Police officer! Freeze!"

Heitkamp squared his shoulders and marched toward the sound of Fraizer's voice. "Glad you're here officer. This man is trespassing.

Fraizer aimed his pistol at Cole as he approached. "I've been following you, mister. I knew you were up to no good." He whipped out a pair of cuffs and slapped them on Cole so quick Cole's mouth was caught open.

Cole had seen Fraizer cuff prisoners before, spinning them around and locking their wrists behind them. He never realized it took so little time.

Fraizer took one finger and gently closed Cole's mouth. "I'll take care of him. You can come down later and sign the complaint."

Cole whispered, "They've got Leslie."

Fraizer said, "It won't do you any good to try to bribe me, mister."

Cole jerked away from Fraizer. "They've kidnapped Leslie, you idiot."

Heitkamp slowly scratched his head. "I can't imagine what he's talking about, officer. If you need any help getting him to your car, Jon will be glad to lend a hand."

Jon nodded. He wasn't grinning anymore. Cole thought he caught a fleeting glimmer of recognition across the redhead's face. The only thing bright about the boy was his hair.

As Fraizer pulled Cole from around behind him, he rammed a fist in his gut. "Oops, sorry, mister. I must've slipped." He grabbed the handcuffs and shoved Cole ahead of him. "No, sir, I don't think I'll have any trouble with him now."

Cole twisted and tried to speak, but Fraizer yanked up on the cuffs. Cole thought his shoulders were going to relocate to somewhere closer to his ears. Then Fraizer dropped the cuffs and grabbed Cole around the shoulders. He squeezed him harder than seemed necessary under the circumstances, but Cole figured it was best to keep his mouth shut.

Fraizer whispered, "Chill out, Mother Frog. Trust me."

It was light enough to follow the faint trail back to the gate. They stayed close to the fence line and ducked low pine branches when Fraizer looked above their knees instead of watching the ground. After the first pine needles slapped their faces, his gaze bounced between the ground and sky. With each bounce, he jerked Cole off the ground.

When they got to the front gate, Cole saw the rope ladder slung over the fence. "What's this, Big Boy? Our man-in-blue a fence climber?"

Fraizer said, "You didn't think about how you were going to get out of there, did you?"

"Just get these damn cuffs off me."

"Not till you promise to be a good boy, Mother Frog."

"I'll be a good boy after I get Leslie out of there!" He turned and shoved his locked wrists toward Fraizer. "Besides, I can't climb a ladder like this."

Like a sudden leak in a radial tire, came the whisper. "Pssst! Roy?"

Fraizer chuckled softly. "Yeah, Rose, let us out."

Cole swaggered toward the gate. He knew Fraizer wasn't going to make him climb the ladder in handcuffs. At least, that's what he told himself.

Fraizer said, "Rose, I owe you. I thought I was going to have to use that damn rope again."

When Fraizer had the rope coiled to throw in his trunk he lumbered up beside Cole and grabbed his arms. The cuffs came off almost as fast as they went on.

Cole rubbed his wrists. "We gotta get Leslie. I'm not going anywhere without her."

A single headlight washed across the gate as it rounded the curve. The motorcycle slowed to a roar. The driver cocked the machine to one side. The passenger behind him was silhouetted, but Cole didn't have any trouble recognizing Leslie.

She trotted toward him. "This is great! Ya'll can take me home. That way I won't have to ride that overgrown sewing machine."

Jon killed the motor. "Mr. Heitkamp said if I could get you to take her home, it would be all right. I'm sorry I didn't recognize you, Mr. January. No offense, I hope."

Cole raised an eyebrow. "None taken, Jon. Hope you folks

had a nice visit." He grabbed Leslie's elbow and pushed her to the patrol car.

Rose said, "No sir. Not me. Roy promised all I had to do before I went on duty was meet him out here with the gate code and back him up if he had any trouble. I got the code from Security and he's out of trouble. I'm gone."

Leslie jerked away from Cole. "Just what the hell do you think you're doing? I am not a child." She stomped to Fraizer's car.

Cole slowly, in one smooth stroke, rubbed his head from his eyebrows to the rim of hair in back. "Big Boy, what am I going to do with her?"

Fraizer unlocked his car and leaned over the top. "I don't think that's your decision, Mother Frog."

Of course it wasn't. It seemed as if nothing was his decision anymore. He didn't even get to decide when he would buy a new car. His shiny red Luv was totaled, and he'd planned to drive it another year. Beneath all his mental meanderings one thought pulsated: He'd never been so sleepy in his whole life. "Let's go home."

They rode in silence until they turned off the freeway and headed up Gessner toward Leslie's house. She leaned forward in the seat and looked at Fraizer. "How did you know to get off at Gessner?"

Neither Cole nor Fraizer answered.

Leslie huffed. "You've been here checking on me, haven't you?"

Cole patted her shoulder from the backseat. "We were just worried about you, honey."

Leslie's voice dropped one notch, slowed down two, and hit every syllable with equal force. "Just two things, Coleman January, and don't you forget 'em. One, I'm not your *honey*, and two, I can take care of myself."

"Is that so?" He poked his chin toward her. "Then what the hell were you doing at Jack Heitkamp's house all night?" Cole didn't want any partner of his fraternizing with the enemy.

Leslie said, "Waiting for Jack and Jon to finish their business so Jon could take me home." She took a deep breath. "You, my charming date, disappeared. I had to lie my ass off to convince them I didn't know anything about your case." She turned in the seat. "You don't look sick to me, but the sight—or is it the smell?—of you is making me sick."

Fraizer pulled into her driveway and was almost stopped when she opened the door and jumped out. "I can see myself to the door, thank you."

Cole crawled out from the backseat and shouted, "We'll talk about this in the morning!"

Leslie spun around. "This *is* morning, you asshole."

Cole wondered why he ever thought they could have more than a working relationship. She was as unpredictable as any other woman. He decided he must have lost his mind with Kevin's impending arrival. Maybe it brought out his family instincts. He decided to give that more thought after he caught up on sleep.

By the time Fraizer dropped Cole at his apartment, Cole was close to being asleep on his feet. A nap in a roadside park could only do so much. He stumbled in through the back gate and hoped he had enough energy to climb the stairs.

The place didn't smell too much like a litterbox anymore. Maybe It had discovered the dishpan with the green stuff in it. Or maybe Cole smelled worse than the litterbox.

Blondie was drifting with her nose near the bottom of the tank, sleeping, he guessed. As he got closer, she swam over to the side and did her version of the twist to get his attention. He couldn't remember if he'd fed her in the past twenty-four hours, so he gave her a couple of pellets.

He had intended to take a shower and hit the sheets, but it was almost noon when he roused and found himself on the sofa, It kneading his chest and purring like a well-tuned lawn mower. In spite of himself, he stroked her before he gently lowered her to the floor. Though he knew she wasn't, he thought of It as Leslie's cat. By the time he was fully awake, he didn't want to think of Leslie at all—except in a business way. He also didn't want to think about who killed whom and who was threatening Molly and why any body was ever found in his apartment.

He hoped to leave business alone long enough to let his subconscious filter through the evidence and head him in the right direction. One mind-occupying task he couldn't avoid anyway would solve his problem.

The mall was always crowded on Saturday afternoon, but it wouldn't make any difference to Cole. All he had to do was find a way to get there. He hated shopping as much as the next man, unless he was shopping for Kevin. Anything with or for Kevin was special, and he knew he could put all his thought and energy into it. He was determined to get the perfect surprise.

For every visit, Cole tried to have a special surprise gift waiting for Kevin when he arrived. He always thought of the gifts as surprises, but Kevin knew they would be there. Not in a greedy way, Cole argued with Linda, but as part of the fun they had together.

As he nibbled at the last stale bagel, Rose popped into his head. He wondered if she had a full shift or if she was pulling a short shift and taking someone in to look at a lineup. He pointed his finger at the cat. "What say I call and find out? After all, what are friends for? And I do owe her at least a meal."

Cole let the phone ring a long time before the machine answered. He didn't leave a message. Maybe he would try again later. He couldn't go anywhere without a shower and shave, anyway.

Feeling as fresh as a virgin on prom night, he walked to the apartment manager's office. Rose still wasn't home and there wasn't anyone else he wanted to impose on.

Ms. Stewart lowered her glasses to the end of her nose and looked up at him. "I hope you're satisfied, Mr. January. We'll never rent another apartment, and we've had six move-outs since that poor girl's body was found in your apartment."

Cole approached her desk cautiously and whispered, "I'm sorry. I didn't do it."

"Momma warned me about the likes of you. Prying in other folk's business is no way to make an honest dollar."

Cole nodded and lowered his voice to impress her with his acknowledgment of the seriousness of the situation. "Yes, ma'am."

As if she hadn't made the previous comments, Ms. Stewart smiled and folded her hands on the desk. "Is there something I can help you with?"

"Yes, ma'am. I'd like to speak with Jennifer Ann."

"You know I can't give you her apartment number."

Cole had been nice as long as he could without effort. His fuse was shorter than on most days, but he took a deep breath. He kept his voice low and forced a smile. "It's kind of important, Ms. Stewart. Could you call her and let me talk to her?"

Ms. Stewart reached for the phone. She looked up at him, then shielded the number pad as she punched in the numbers.

Jennifer Ann agreed to meet him in front of his apartment if he promised not to take too much of her time. She was on her way to Play-Lanes Bowling Alley, and she didn't want to be late for the big tournament.

Standing beside his apartment door, Cole watched her approach. If he didn't know it was the same girl he'd seen in the manager's office, he'd never suspect it. Her snug jeans and baggy T-shirt, little or no makeup, and hair pulled back in combs made her look young enough to be his daughter.

Jennifer Ann stopped in front of him and slid her sunglasses to the top of her head. "I swear I didn't tell anybody about your stereo or that you talked to me. Now, can I go?"

Cole smiled. "Good girl. But it's okay. I need to know if you remembered anything else about the man that got the key."

Jennifer Ann shook her head. "Mostly, I've tried to not

think about it. I figure the stereo delivery men must have left the door open, and somebody just dumped the body in your place 'cause it was open."

"Jennifer Ann," Cole said in what he hoped was a fatherly tone, "the stereo *was* the body. Do you remember anything at—"

Jennifer Ann sucked in a big breath and expelled her words. "Ohmygod! Ohmygod! Why can't I remember? I've gotta remember. Ohmygod!" She bounced and shook her hands. She stopped, blanched white, and rolled her eyes.

Cole thought she was going to faint. He grabbed her shoulders. "Jennifer Ann. Chill out!" Ms. Stewart would never forgive him if she fainted. "Breathe," he begged.

"I'm okay," she mumbled. She stepped away from him and dug around in her handbag until she came up with a pack of Virginia Slims. Her hands were shaking so hard, the flame from the purple plastic lighter didn't catch the tip of the cigarette until the third try.

After she exhaled the first billow of smoke, she very slowly said, "He was big. I know he was big. He wasn't blond, but he didn't have real dark hair, either. I'm sure of that, but the light wasn't so good." She shook her head. Her eyes looked as if she were trying to focus on the memory. "I should have had all the lights on." Looking up at Cole, she shrugged. "The TV is clearer if the office isn't so bright."

Cole said, "I understand. When we first talked, you said he was a jock. What made you think that?"

She grinned. "The muscles. He had great muscles. And buns. I always notice a nice set of buns."

Cole reached for his doorknob. "That's what I wanted to know. Thanks, Jennifer Ann. You've been a big help."

Jennifer Ann squealed. "Gee! Really?"

She looked as if she were going to knock him off his feet again. He jumped into his apartment. "Yeah, really."

Cole dialed Mid-Town Gym. Each time he got a busy signal, he chewed on a pretzel while he dialed again. He had to get food in the place for Kevin, too, he realized.

When Hacksaw finally came on the line, Cole said, "Can I get in to see Jimmy if I can find a way over there?"

Hacksaw said, "I just got through talking to him. He's out of lockup. What do you mean if you can find a way over there?"

Cole grunted. "Some jerk ran me off the road and totaled my truck. I got it towed to town, but I know it's totaled. Leslie'll take me to get a loaner car in the morning."

Hacksaw said, "I can send you a car if you don't care what it looks like. My brother-in-law has a rent-a-heap business over on Washington Avenue."

While he waited for the car to arrive, Cole opened the sofa bed and put on fresh sheets. As long as he had to hang around the apartment, he figured he may as well get some chores out of the way. He had the pillow tucked under his chin and was scooting the case up the sides when he remembered.

He dropped the pillow and grabbed the phone. Shopping for Kevin would have to wait. Molly wasn't home, but Jon was. He gave Cole very good directions.

▽

8

THE DARK-BLUE Chevy Caprice looked older than it was, but it wasn't new. Someone had raked the right side more than once. The side mirror and rear wheel well were caved in. It backfired for the third time as Cole turned into the driveway at the home of Judith Barnes.

The lawn definitely required more maintenance than Leslie's. The sculptured hedges and terraced flower beds looked to Cole as if they kept a crew busy all year. Probably at the city's expense, he thought.

If he was right, Judith had set him up at the barbecue, and probably planted the "bomb" under Molly's car, too. What all this had to do with the murder was anybody's guess. But all's fair in love and war—and politics. The way Cole had it figured, Judith wasn't about to lose the campaign *and* her boyfriend. As crazy as she'd acted at Olsen's blowout, she might be crazy enough to kill.

The tape on the picture window across the front of Judith's house looked fresh. Was a hurricane headed for Galveston Bay without him knowing it? Very unlikely, he decided, since none of the other houses on the block were taped or boarded up. Cole couldn't imagine why Judith would tape up one window. It didn't look cracked, and none of the glass was missing.

The other thing that worried him was that he wasn't exactly sure what he would say to Judith. The last time he had seen her she was slightly hysterical. Hopefully, after she discovered that Jack hadn't dropped her for Leslie, she would be properly remorseful and welcome him. Then again, she might not. Playing hunches was something he usually avoided, but at this point, he didn't have anything else.

As if she'd been standing there with her hand on the door, Judith immediately threw it open. "Thank God, you're here!" She stretched up on her tiptoes and looked past him. "Where are the police? Don't tell me they didn't take me seriously!"

Cole stepped back. "Sorry, I don't see any police, and I haven't got the vaguest idea what you're talking about. What say you start at the top."

Judith grabbed his arm and pulled him into the house. "Don't stand out there. They might see you."

Cole turned to look behind him just as she slammed the door. "They who?"

"Can't you see?" She pointed at the front window.

What Cole saw was a large birdcage holding a white cockatoo in front of the double windows. Dark-maroon drapes flanked the sheer curtains over the taped left window. He pointed. "You have tape on your window."

"Because they tried to kill me. They shot through the window and tried to kill me!"

The conversation wasn't at all going in the direction Cole had in mind. If she was a victim, it probably took her out of the suspect column. He softened his voice to abate her hysteria. "Judith, who tried to kill you? Did you see anyone?"

"Oh, don't be a fool. Of course I didn't see anyone. Do you think they would let me see them?" She huffed her way to the wet bar and unstopped a decanter that was three quarters full of Scotch. She lifted it toward Cole. "Would you care for a drink?"

"No, ma'am, none for me, thank you. But you go ahead. I'm sure you're a bit rattled."

"Damn right, I'm rattled. You would be, too, if they were after you." She paced the length of the room, then stopped in front of him. She looked past him out the window. "Where the hell are the damn police when you need them?" She drank half the tumbler of Scotch. "And what the hell are you doing here?"

Cole had no idea what he was doing there, but he remembered why it was iffy to play a hunch. "I . . . I just wanted to thank you for the tickets. That was nice of you to get them for us."

He backed toward the door. "Nice. Thank you. I'll just let myself out."

Judith walked back to the decanter and refilled her glass. "If you see the police, tell them I'm alive. Not that they give a damn." She tossed off a good bit of the drink. "They'll burn in hell before they get another raise, too."

Cole couldn't get to the rent-a-heap fast enough. All his ideas were backfiring as loudly as the old Chevy. At least the car got him to the parking lot that bordered the west side of Misty Glen Psychiatric Hospital. At least this wasn't a trip on a hunch, it was to see a suspect who had motive, ability, and quite possibly, opportunity.

The television commercials for "The Glen" depicted plush gardens, tennis courts, a swimming pool, and reunited families. Cole thought the vacation spas of the world should take lessons from the Misty Glen public relations department on how to attract visitors. The commercials never mentioned lockup, detox, or shock treatments.

Cole's name was not on the visitor list the young receptionist scanned on the monitor in front of her. She looked up. "I'm sorry, Mr. January, only family or names on the list."

Cole rubbed the back of his neck. "Gosh, ma'am, I'm sure Little Jimmy didn't expect his half brother to be in town. I been driving for mite near six hours. Reckon you could check with him?"

The young woman raised an eyebrow. "Little Jimmy? Are you sure you've got the right man?"

"Oh, yes ma'am. We call him Little Jimmy 'cause he's a junior. Momma called his daddy Big Jimmy."

She sighed and pressed the door-lock release. "Go on back. He's in the day room."

Cole bowed slightly. "Thank you kindly, ma'am." He guessed he hadn't overdone the East Texas twang.

Jimmy "The Strangler" Strauss should have been easy to pick out of the twenty or so patients and visitors in the day room, but there were four large men in sight. One was holding a three-year-old boy on his lap; another was more likely a teenager than a man. That left the one reading beside the lamp in the corner and the one playing Ping-Pong. Both men had long brownish hair, were about the right age, and were iron-pumping, steroid-eating big.

Cole started toward the Ping-Pong player. When he reached the corner of the table, he stopped and watched until the hulk slammed the ball off the edge. While the opponent scrambled after the ball, Cole said, "I need to talk to you."

The man looked at Cole like he was wondering if it was safe to talk to him. He looked over his shoulder at his partner, then back at Cole. "Who the hell are you?"

Cole stuck out his hand. "Cole January. I'm a friend of—"

The other player shouted. "Heads up, Bill. Here comes a sizzler."

Cole grinned. "We can talk after you're finished, Bill."

Cole wished he'd paid more attention to the sports magazines or gotten a picture from Hacksaw. Tentatively, he sat down on the other end of the sofa from the man reading the dark-blue book. The man's lips didn't move as he read, but the strained expression on his face indicated he was struggling with the words. Like an animal that senses a trap, Jimmy looked up.

Cole didn't want to scare him off. Very softly, he said, "Hacksaw said you're feeling much better."

Jimmy's smile looked more like a puncture in his bloated face. "You know Hacksaw?"

Cole leaned back on the couch and cocked his ankle on the opposite knee. "Yeah, we go way back." A couple of months, at least, he thought.

Jimmy leaned toward Cole and whispered. "You tell that motherfucker to get me out of here."

"Whoa, Jimmy, I got no stroke with this place or Hacksaw. I just want to have a friendly little chat." He glanced around the room. "Is there somewhere sort of private we can go?"

Jimmy slowly placed the book on the end table, then turned to Cole. "Depends. What do you want to have this friendly little chat about?"

"Oh, I don't know. Maybe you could tell me about a lady friend of yours. Molly Jones-Heitkamp. You know anything about her, Jimmy?"

Jimmy slipped the book back into his lap and opened it. "Got nothing to say about Molly."

Cole said, "I think you do, Jimmy. You want me to get the police in here?"

Jimmy rubbed the bruised knuckles of his left hand. When he stood up, he looked like an adult getting up from a child's sofa. He started toward the door without looking back.

Cole followed. When he passed the Ping-Pong players, the big one said, "I'll be with you after this game."

Cole smiled. "Take your time, Bill. I'll catch you later."

In the hall, Jimmy said, "You know Bill?"

"Never saw him before in my life."

Jimmy said, "You got me all confused, man. I gotta think." He pushed through the double doors that led to the wing of private rooms.

Cole said, "Take your time, Jimmy. I can be very patient."

The receptionist from the front desk swished past them. "I see you found your brother."

Jimmy said, "I don't have no—"

Cole jumped in front of Jimmy. "Yes, ma'am. We're doing just fine."

She was through the double doors and out of earshot when Jimmy said, "I wondered how you got in here. Did Hacksaw tell you to say you're my brother?"

Cole grinned cockily. "No sir, I thought it up all by myself."

"I don't know if I can trust you—what'd you say your name is?"

"Cole, Cole January." He pulled a business card from his pocket and handed it to Jimmy.

Jimmy shook his head, then leaned against the wall and stared down at the card. "I knew it; I knew it. You're trouble looking for a place to happen. Well, it's not going to happen here." He slapped the card against Cole's chest. "Get the fuck out of here!"

Cole wasn't used to psych patients telling him what to do. So far, he didn't like it. He also wasn't used to looking for murderers. So far, he didn't like that either. Considering that Jimmy may have killed a woman, a very attractive woman, it seemed likely to Cole that he wouldn't hesitate to break a few bones of a bald-headed man. That would not only ruin Kevin's visit, it would be painful.

Cole was not fond of pain in any of his body parts. What happened to all the big insurance fraud cases, and why wasn't he out there solving one of them? he wondered. Surely someone in Houston had burned down his own building or faked an injury recently.

Somewhere between returning Cole's business card and reaching his room, something happened in Jimmy's head. He pushed open the door to Room 181. "Aw, what the fuck. You're here. What do you want?"

Cole sighed and entered the small room. "Nice," he said.

It was small, but far from the simple decor Cole expected. The designer spread, custom drapes, and mirrored vanity were all top of the line. Beside the bed was an entertainment center, complete with CD, TV, VCR, and any other initials Cole could think of. The wood cabinet didn't match the rest of the furniture. Cole wondered if Jimmy brought it with him, or if the hospital provided it for their celebrity patients. He made a mental note to check one of the other rooms on his way out.

The only window in the room was large and overlooked a courtyard filled with trees, periwinkles, and benches. The late-afternoon sun caught the gurgling fountain on the far side of the enclosure and sprinkled diamonds in the blue-tinted water. Cole watched a sparrow splash in the birdbath while other birds sat on the rim as if waiting their turn.

As he dropped into the plush chair near the door, he glimpsed a fluffy squirrel tail as its bearer circled the nearest tree trunk. "Very nice," he said. "A fellow could get a lot of rest in a place like this."

Jimmy turned on him. "I damn sure didn't come here for a rest. Cut to the chase."

Cole said, "The scene goes likes this. Someone killed a woman who looks a lot like Molly Jones-Heitkamp. Molly thinks you had reason to want her dead. Where were you late Wednesday night and early Thursday morning?"

A pained expression crossed Jimmy's face and echoed in his voice. "I wouldn't never want Molly dead. I don't care if she did shit on me. Not dead."

"Oh, I want to believe you, Jimmy. But where were you? Do you remember?"

▽

9

THE BIG WRESTLER melted like a snow cone in August, slowly, drip by drop, until his bulk was a puddle in the middle of his bed. His legs were folded Indian-style; his face was buried in his hands. He mumbled something Cole couldn't understand, his shoulders bouncing with silent sobs.

Cole hated to see a grown man cry, especially one as big as Jimmy. Even more, he hated to disturb the wrestler while he was in such obvious pain.

After a few more racking, bouncing sobs, Jimmy smeared his tears away with the pillow and turned his streaked face toward Cole. "Did you hear me?" he shouted. "I said I don't know! How do you like that tune?" He slapped the pillow across the room. "I don't fucking know!"

Cole nodded as if he understood and was mustering up some help. Cole had never been too delicate in awkward situations. Part of his brain told him if he said the wrong thing, Jimmy would freeze up and not tell him if he did remember anything. The other part claimed it didn't make any difference what he said; Jimmy was nuts. His usual response was to attack, but for the time being he went with his better judgment. On the outside chance that Jimmy could pull himself together, Cole said, "Maybe it'll come to you. What's the last thing you remember?"

Jimmy held up his hands. "Okay, okay." Hugging his knees to his chest, he said, "It was like this, man—what's your name?"

"January. Cole January."

"Aw, man, you're shittin' me." He almost grinned. "Okay, so Cold January or Hot July or whoever the fuck you are." A half-giggle bounced out his nostrils, but his big, bulging eyes showed no merriment. "I was with this lady, see. We were doing Cherry's Lounge. The place was too quiet, so—"

"Cherry's? Is that the place over by—"

"Shut up! I'm trying to think."

Cole's hackles raised. No mutant gorilla numb-brain could tell him to shut up and live. Then he realized where he was and locked his lips. Inside a nut farm was no place for ultimatums. He watched the muscle jerk in Jimmy's left hand.

Cole thought Jimmy may have been a fair-looking specimen at one time, as far as mutant gorillas go. But some match had ended with part of one ear missing. His nose had been broken more than once and never stabilized. It roamed across his face like a buffalo working its way between two hills. Cole wondered if the price of fame was worth mangled looks and the anguish Jimmy was suffering now.

Did wrestling screw up his head, or did he wrestle because it was already screwed up? Either way, Cole felt sorry for him. If he were the murderer, he didn't know it. Cole was convinced of that.

Jimmy threw himself back on the bed. His head hung off the far side from Cole; his feet dangled near Cole's shins.

Cole waited a minute, maybe two, then said, "What say I come back tomorrow?"

Jimmy kicked his feet over his head and landed on the floor, facing Cole. "Wait!" His eyes were shiny with leftover tears. "I was at LeBistro, over off Kirby. Maggie was there. And Vicki. Maybe they know where we went when we left there."

His eyes were unfocused as he looked at the distant image. "Yeah," he breathed. "Ask 'em. You'll see. I didn't kill nobody."

Cole nodded. "Sure. I'll ask them. Maggie and Vicki. If you think of anything else, let me know."

Cole backed out of the room, glad to go. Nut wards gave him the creeps. Calling them "treatment centers" didn't change the fact that the patients were mentally unstable. It only put a label on them. Alcoholic, manic-depressive, OCD, paranoid—it all meant nuts. He stayed away from them every chance he got. Not that he'd been in that many.

The only psychiatric hospital he could remember since he visited his aunt Becky with his mother when he was ten was when he went to see one of his first clients at the county nut farm.

That Ross kid had been sent through a psychiatric evaluation before Cole had been allowed to talk to him. Cole had been admitted to his room before Ross was returned to the jail.

Any trip to any nuthouse was more than Cole wanted. It was a rotten way to spend a Saturday afternoon. He hoped he wouldn't have to come back tomorrow.

When the old Chevy backfired, it sounded like a .22 fired about three inches from Cole's ear. He jumped and involuntarily jerked the wheel. He was grateful there wasn't much traffic on the side street.

It was a different story when he entered the freeway. Cole thought the amber mercury lights that lined the Southwest Freeway looked like a splendid serpent snaking its way toward downtown Houston. The outbound lanes were thick with cars, campers, and boats returning from the far side of the city to the suburbs. Come Monday morning, they'd leave their playtoys in the garage, or in a storage shed, or beside the house. Bleary-eyed, they'd jockey for a place on the freeway in front of Cole so they could work their buns off all week—so they could play another weekend.

If all the travelers had stayed home, he could have gotten to LeBistro in half the time. He swung to the inside lane to pass a Blazer pulling a twenty-five-foot Wellcraft. The traffic wasn't moving any faster in that lane. If Cole loved the lakes or bays as much as some folks said they did, he'd find a way to live there if he had to dig worms or cull shrimp. Instead, he sat behind them while they inched along in front of him across the serpent's back and dreamed of a place on the water.

As Cole dropped off the freeway at Kirby, he bid the serpent good-bye and wondered if LeBistro was still where he remembered. The last time he was there was before he met Linda. He realized he should have called. Bars in Houston open, close, and move more often than crap games. He seldom went into bars, unless it was necessary for a case he was working on. He had no intention of ending up like Aunt Becky.

He hadn't gone out at all for eight or ten months after the divorce. He had wondered if he would ever trust his soul to another woman. The pain of loneliness got worse than the fear, and he realized casual dating wasn't a commitment. When he did start dating again, he generally took a lady out for dinner and dancing or a concert or a play. There weren't many entertainers he'd buck the traffic to see in concert anymore, but he'd developed a reputation for picking good plays—with Henrietta's help.

Cole expected LeBistro to still be the small, classy place with velvet wallpaper and intimate music that it had been. He knew the smoke would be thick enough to slice, and the owner, gray-haired by now, would welcome him with that thick French accent. Subtle lighting over the old Toulouse-Lautrec prints wouldn't interfere with the soft glow of candles on each table. The candles would be the same ones he remembered, with a dozen years of candle drippings added down the sides of the cheap wine bottles. Maybe he'd have a glass of wine while he talked to the two ladies.

A flashing arrow on the corner of the building still pointed the way to the back door of the one-story structure—the main entrance for LeBistro customers.

Cole opened the door and barged into bright lights, cameras, and action. A wedding reception was being recorded for future generations. His mood shattered, he approached the nearest server, who was decked out in the customary little black dress with white apron and cap. "I'm looking for Maggie or Vicki. I was told they work here."

The woman smiled. "Not today, cutie. What's your name, and I'll tell them you came by."

"Just say a friend of Jimmy Strauss's. I'll check back tomorrow." Cole saw a glint of recognition for the name, then a frozen mask.

"You may not be welcome when you show up. If I were you, I'd pick my friends a bit more carefully." She scooped an empty glass and wadded napkin from a table.

Cole thought she was going to say something more, but she scooted through the knot of people at the piano, gathering more debris en route to the kitchen.

He weaved his way through the clusters of well-wishers to the rest rooms. At least the same black pay phone hugged the wall near the corner.

Since he couldn't accomplish what he set out to do, he'd do something else, even if he couldn't think of any reason why he should. He bounced his fingers across the numbers, then drummed on the wall until the ringing stopped.

"Leslie, I'm sorry. I apologize."

"I guess I was a mite bitchy. But, Cole, please don't patronize me."

"It won't happen again."

"Okay. 'Bye."

"No! Wait! I'm . . . uh . . . going out to Wal-Mart to buy some stuff for Kevin. Want to come along?" As long as he had to fight traffic, he may as well have company doing it. It sounded like a good reason to him.

In less than an hour Cole and Leslie were walking through the toy department aisles for the third time. Cole was aware that Leslie's praises for his selections had stopped. She had voted for the Teenage Mutant Ninja Turtle figures and the jazzy skateboard. She sort of okayed the Battle Beasts and Trolls, but was cool toward the indoor Nerf basketball setup. He fingered several items without any response. When he picked up the Daisy BB rifle, she stopped in midstride and stared at him.

"What's the matter?"

Leslie folded her arms across her chest. "Don't you think you've got enough?"

Cole said, "You're no fun. I was just getting warmed up." He put the gun back in the rack. "But you're right. I always get too much. Besides, I think I got him a BB gun last summer." And if he didn't, he and Kevin could always come back.

While they were queued up at the checkout counter, Leslie said, "Cole, I'm having some trouble piecing together what I've got on my missing person. Could we go over it in the morning?"

"Just tell Papa what you've got, and Papa'll make it all better."

She kept her voice low, but her tone shouted. "Damn it, Cole, you're doing it again! I just asked for a little help. I need to talk it through, and you talk down to me like I'm some helpless bimbo."

"Okay, okay. I get the message. We'll go over it. You've probably missed some little something that doesn't sound important." He knew that's what was bogging down his case. Some minor, insignificant piece of information that he already had but didn't know it.

Leslie helped him unload the shopping cart. "You may have the message, but that didn't sound like an apology to me."

By the time they got to the car, Cole had apologized sufficiently to appease her. He wondered if it was his imagination or if she was especially touchy. This was a new nettle, and he kept getting stung.

When they stopped at the Toddle House for coffee, she was more like her old self—wrapped up in her work and eager to learn more. Cole was puzzled. He didn't know if he had said or done something to elicit the change or if it was spontaneous. He didn't ask. Whatever it was, he liked it.

Leslie stirred her coffee and looked across the table at him. "I don't know if I've got two missing women or if Janice Phillips and Karren Janson are the same person."

Cole said, "You got a match on the Social Security number, didn't you?"

"Yes, but—"

"So what's the problem? Do you think Kevin will like the skateboard?"

She managed to get three syllables in his name. "Cole! I'm trying to talk to you. Pay attention."

"Okay, so you got two names, one missing woman. And I've got a cat I don't want. What's your next move?"

"Go back and see if the landlady will let me in her apartment?"

"Bravo! Now, what do you really think about the Turtles? Too young?"

By the time they finished their coffee, both seemed satisfied. Leslie promised to find a home for the cat and assured him the gifts for Kevin were perfect. Cole promised to fully review her case Monday and assured her he wouldn't buy anything else for Kevin.

After he dropped her off, the long drive to his apartment gave him time to sort through what he knew on his own case. The Molly Jones-Heitkamp Case was developing more facets than a diamond display at Dillard's. Come Monday morning, Molly would be expecting answers he didn't yet have.

He still didn't have any answers after a solid night's sleep, but his energy was back to normal levels. He got in his three miles at the Memorial Park track before he settled down and outlined what he had so far. The rest of the day, he did the chores he hated: laundry, straightening, and commode-scrubbing. Until Linda left, he never knew how much work it took to keep a place clean. As soon as he could afford it, he planned to hire a maid.

By Monday, he was ready to get back to work, but he had to tell Henrietta about all the toys first. He bounded through the office door. "Henrietta! Guess what I got for Kevin."

There was no answer.

Thinking maybe she was back in Leslie's office, he rounded the corner and jerked the door open.

She wasn't there.

He looked at his watch—9:08. He went back to her desk and yanked up the telephone. He punched in the voice-mail number. Nothing. The phone hadn't been rolled over. Then he remembered. He'd aborted the transfer Friday night. Cursing himself under his breath, he stomped into his office.

He flipped through his card file and found Henrietta's home number. No answer.

Just as he hung up, the phone rang.

Rose Johnson said, "Roy said for you to sit tight. He thinks he's found out who whacked you at the gym."

Sitting tight with Henrietta unaccounted for was not easy. The longer the case lasted, the more he knew he preferred live people to dead ones. Solving murders took a special caliber of investigator. He didn't think he was that caliber, and he knew he didn't want to be. There was too much to worry about.

He called Henrietta's house again and again, with the same results. By 9:45 he was ready to roll the phone and go over there. He had a mental picture of her on the floor, unable to get to her chair or the phone. He worried about her living alone anyway, and her absence gave credence to his worry.

While he worried and waited, he went over his list of facts and hunches. After his experience with Judith, he wasn't too keen on hunches. Without the hunches, he was down to very few facts, and none pointing in the same direction. It might come down to playing a hunch after all. He wished he had more to report to Molly.

Cole knew someone was with her before she made it obvious. He said, "If this is a bad time, I could call back later."

Molly took a deep breath. "That would be preferable. Say eleven o'clock?"

"Sounds dandy." Surely by then he'd locate Henrietta and find out what Fraizer knew.

Cole had crossed out over half his hunches when Fraizer banged on the door and opened it. "Does the name Nathan Andrews mean anything?"

Cole walked toward him, scratching his head. "No, not that I can think of."

"How 'bout Hoss?"

"Hoss? That clean-cut, all-American boy I met at the gym?"

"You pegged him, all right. Hasn't bathed in six weeks, never had a haircut in his life, and may have burned a flag or two." Fraizer dropped into the chair beside Henrietta's desk. "He also has a record as long as my leg."

Cole glanced down at Fraizer's legs stretched out in front of him. An impressive length for anything. "What sort of record?"

"Aggravated assault, three counts. Dismissed. Two counts of destruction of public property. Fined. One public intoxication and one possession of a controlled substance. Cocaine. He beat them both on a technicality. Suspected of steroid abuse—"

"And I thought he was just another pretty face." Cole sat on the edge of Henrietta's desk. "What makes you think he's the one who jumped me?"

"He told me, more or less. Said he 'took care' of the last guy sniffing around. Didn't want anybody poking their nose in his or Jimmy's business." Fraizer pulled his feet in and sat up straight. "He never said a word about you or exactly how he took care of anybody. It's not enough to pick him up."

Cole went to his desk and picked up the list he'd been working on. He wasn't sure where to put Hoss, but he definitely belonged on the list. He scribbled the name under "facts" before he carried it back to Fraizer. "This is what I've got. Not much of it fits together, but somehow it's all linked. I've just got to figure out how and who. If Molly Jones-Heitkamp and the dead woman in my bedroom don't have anything to do with each other, it's one of the strangest coincidences in my life."

Fraizer scanned the list and looked up at Cole. "You might want to let Harris in on this. He's gonna be plenty pissed if he finds out you're withholding info."

"I promise I'll get with him as soon as I can." He glanced at his watch.

Fraizer looked around the room and cocked his head to one side. "Where's your SS drill sergeant?"

Cole said, "I don't know. I'm wor—"

Henrietta eased the door open and wheeled in wearing a satisfied grin.

Cole shouted, "Where the hell have you been?"

She didn't cringe or apologize. "I could ask you the same question. I'd have left you a message if I could have."

Cole said, "I'm sorry about the mix-up with Leslie Friday night. She's thoroughly chastised me."

"I talked to her. Forget it." She patted the stack of papers anchored under her purse. "Wait till you see what I've got."

She whipped the wheels of her chair and pivoted around the corner of her desk. After she dropped her purse into the bottom desk drawer, she officially went to work. One by one she slapped the papers on the desk like a short-order cook slapping hamburger patties on a grill. With the photocopies spread out, Henrietta pointed to each of the newspaper articles. "Every one of these looks like Molly, but some of them aren't."

Cole picked up one of the sheets and scrutinized the blurred picture. "How can you tell?"

Fraizer got to his feet and straightened his tie. "Haven't you ever heard of celebrity stand-ins? All the big stars have them."

Cole smirked. "I'd hardly call Molly Jones-Heitkamp a big star."

Fraizer rocked back on his heels. "I remember one time I thought I'd busted Chevy Chase. 'Course, when he got out of the car I saw how short he was and I knew—"

Henrietta held up one of the copies. "This one is the best. Look real close."

Cole strode to his desk and came back with a small magnifying glass. Peering at the copy through the glass, he said, "So? What am I looking for?"

"The teeth. See how that one has a small split between her front teeth? Not big. Just a little different." She held another page toward him. "Now look at this one."

Fraizer looked over Cole's shoulder and let out a low whistle. "Who is she?"

Cole tossed the paper back on the desk. "That's what I intend to find out."

▽

10

"THANK GOD YOU called, Cole. You've got to meet me at Ruben's. How soon can you be here?"

Cole made motions toward Henrietta that he needed paper and pen. She scooted them toward him as he said, "What say you tell me where Mr. Gomez lives, then I can tell you how quick I can get there."

Molly's voice was back to the panicky tones he'd first heard. She gave him sketchy directions and an address not far from her home. "Cole," she sniffed, "please hurry!"

Cole replaced the receiver and stared at the wall.

Fraizer said, "Okay, Mother Frog, what gives?"

Henrietta pulled a Bugs Bunny. "Heh, what's up, Doc?"

Cole said, "She wants me to meet her at Ruben Gomez's. Fraizer, I swear I'll call Harris the first chance I get."

Fraizer said, "He's gonna want to see those copies."

"I'll go see him. I'll take the damn copies." He swiveled toward Henrietta. "And you tell Leslie I'll go over her case with her when I get back. And here"—he handed her the photocopies—"make copies for him while I get my stuff together."

The dark-blue Chevy had soaked up more sun than a Coppertone billboard. He was within three blocks of Ruben's when the air conditioner finally cooled the car. It wasn't that he didn't appreciate Hacksaw getting him a drivable vehicle on short notice, but next time, he promised himself, he'd call Hertz or Avis.

With a name like Ruben Gomez, Cole expected to find

pink plastic flamingos in the flower beds. Instead, he found manicured hedges bordered with white periwinkles. The wrought-iron letters *RG* stood out from the dark bricks of the chimney that rose above the gables. Ruben's Old English home was as far from flamingos as the Astros were from the pennant.

Cole parked in the wide brick driveway, which passed under an arch of oak branches before it wound its way to the garage.

The doorbell was set in the intercom panel beside the door. Cole pushed it twice and waited. He could hear voices, but couldn't make out the words. He pushed it again just as a woman's voice blared from the speaker. "Keep your breeches on!"

Cole grinned. Whoever she was, she didn't sound afraid of anything or anybody.

When the door opened, a petite woman not more than five feet tall stared up at Cole. Her coal-black eyes sized him up quickly as friend, not enemy. Otherwise, Cole was sure she'd have no trouble slamming the door on him.

She pushed a lock of heavy black hair behind her left ear. "You the guy Ruben say is to come here?"

Her English was better than Cole's Spanish. He smiled and bowed slightly. "Yes, ma'am. Mr. Gomez is expecting me."

"You no be too long? I get the coffees." She turned and padded on bare feet across the marble foyer.

It wasn't until she turned around that Cole saw her hair was long enough for her to sit on. Her soft curves were not hidden by the swaying hair. Cole grinned to himself. He might find more than murder clues in Candidate Gomez's casa.

He followed the swaying hair toward the voices. As they crossed the den, he recognized Molly's voice. From its pitch, he surmised she was still on the tense side of panic. The man, presumably Ruben Gomez, was trying to soothe her. His dulcet tones might calm a wild beast or a savage señorita, but were having no effect on Ms. Molly Jones-Heitkamp.

The woman Cole was following tapped lightly on the door frame. *"El señor está."*

Gomez whispered, "English, Lupe, *por favor.*" He marched to the doorway and beamed. "Come in, Mr. January. Molly and I believe there are some recent developments that merit your attention."

There was no hint in Ruben's speech that any of his ancestors had ever been south of the Rio Grande. If anything, his formal words were draped in the neutral accent of the Midwest and flowered by old-world formalities. He was about the same physical size as Cole, with strong Spanish coloring and sensuous good looks. Cole could see why the polls indicated he was pulling the women's attention, if not always their votes.

Cole smiled at Molly. "I see you're still in one piece."

"I'm not sure for how much longer." The strain in her voice, the tear-streaked makeup, the slump to her shoulders, said more than her words. She didn't move away from the bookcase she leaned against, but looked down and picked at a chipped fingernail as if it were her life's work.

Gomez slapped a hand on Cole's shoulder and guided him toward a blue velvet wingback chair, one of two that faced a leather-inlaid coffee table. Across from the chairs was a brocade sofa, its exposed wood polished to a soft patina.

As they approached the sitting area, Gomez held out his hand toward Molly. "Come, Molly. Join us. It's far too difficult to shout across the room."

Molly looked up and shrugged. "You always get your way, don't you?"

Gomez smiled one of those you-know-how-women-are smiles and said in a half-whispered aside to Cole, "She's not feeling well, but she will cooperate."

Cole wasn't sure what the first trigger was, but his dislike for Gomez was set off and growing. Something about his attitude. In spite of his sophistication, Gomez still reeked of machismo. If Leslie thought Cole patronized her, she'd have a stranglehold on Gomez before introductions were over.

Slowly, Molly wandered more than walked to the sofa. As she sat down, she slipped her shoes off and drew her feet up under her. "I'm very frightened, Cole. I should have trusted you from the beginning."

Ruben pointed to her handbag on the floor. "Don't you think you should show it to him first?"

Molly jerked one shoulder up in a half-shrug. "Now or later. It doesn't matter."

She slipped her feet to the floor and leaned forward. The bag was just beyond her reach. As she stretched to get it, Ruben pushed it toward her with his toe. "This is very difficult for her."

Cole assumed he meant the situation, not retrieving the purse. He nodded and watched Molly pull a folded sheet of paper from the leather bag.

She held it out to him. "This came in the mail this morning."

There was no point in handling it with care. Whatever prints or clues it may have contained were already lost. The words were cut from a slick magazine and stuck to a blank sheet of typing paper with Scotch tape: "Get out of his life or pay the price."

Cole tossed the paper on the coffee table. "Whose life?"

Ruben slowly rose. "Mr. January, it should be obvious that the sender of this threat wants me not only to lose the mayoral race, but to abandon the woman I love. If word of this incident were leaked to the media, what sort of man do you suppose this city would consider me to be?"

Cole looked up at him. He could see Gomez's point, but if Molly's life were in danger, surely he would change his opinion. "Is this the only threat since the bomb?"

Ruben raised his right eyebrow slightly. "Bomb? Molly, is this true?"

Molly nodded. "I didn't want to worry you."

"Worry me! You are threatened by a bomb and you don't tell me? What else have you not told me?"

Molly dropped her hands to her lap. "Nothing. I didn't want you to worry. That's all."

Cole knew how Ruben felt. He'd also wondered what other

lies Molly had told. Trying to piece events together in his mind, Cole stood and walked toward the fireplace. He'd always wanted to perch one foot on a hearth and rest his elbow on a mantel like a movie star, maybe Cary Grant or Rock Hudson. He got his foot up, but quickly realized he was not tall enough to put his elbow on the mantel, so he leaned forward with his elbow on his knee. Not exactly the image he had in mind.

He looked at Gomez. "She didn't want you to worry, Ruben. Don't you think that if her life is in danger, maybe you should worry? Maybe drop out of the race? Or is it worth the price she will pay?"

Ruben jumped to his feet. "And let scum run this city? No! You will be well paid to protect Molly and discover who is making threats against her. That is your job. My job is to win the race for mayor of Houston."

Cole left his awkward position and returned to the sitting area. Maybe he should go back to serving citations and looking for runaways. Murder wasn't nearly as much fun as he'd imagined. He stopped beside Molly. Of course, serving citations didn't put him in touch with the Mollys of the world. He touched her shoulder. "What do *you* want?"

Molly patted the sofa beside her. When Cole sat down, she said, "I want Ruben to win. He'll be a good mayor. I don't want to be killed. Can you protect me? Can you promise I won't get killed? Can you find whoever is threatening me?"

Cole looked into her blue-blue eyes. Something was lurking there. Some veiled threat or promise? Some secret? "I can't promise to protect you, but I'll have a much better chance if you'll tell me everything. If you're keeping anything from me, now is the time to let me know."

Molly sighed. The resignation dripped from her words. "I'm not the apple of Daddy's eye, no matter what he told you. Also, I know he's been seeing Judith more for personal reasons than city business."

Cole said, "You mean Judith Barnes?"

"Yes, the Judith R. Barnes of Rosemary Townsend fame."

He didn't know if now was the time to tell her, but he barged ahead. "Someone fired at her through her front window. Whatever's going on, she's as much a target as you are."

"Maybe," Molly snapped. "Maybe not. She's still after Daddy to marry her. She thinks I'm the reason he won't."

"Are you?" He could imagine that Molly Jones-Heitkamp could make it quite difficult for Judith if she had a mind to.

Ruben cleared his throat. "Mr. January, what two adults decide is not based on what a grown daughter may prefer. Nor is it pertinent that some random hooligan sent a bullet through Ms. Barnes's window."

Cole did not acknowledge Ruben, but kept his eyes on Molly. "Well?"

Molly had not visibly reacted to Ruben's comment, but now she got to her feet and walked to the bookshelves. Stroking the shelves the way she had at her own house seemed to give her strength. "Daddy would stand to lose a lot if he married her."

Cole ran his hand back across his head. He was very confused. "Do you mean he'd lose you? The campaign? What?"

"Let's just say he'd lose a lot that he holds very dear." Molly crossed the room and stood beside Ruben's chair. She pasted a celebrity smile across her face. "Don't you think we make a handsome couple?"

The contrast of his dark good looks with her fair beauty did indeed make for a handsome couple, but Cole failed to see what that had to do with the present problems. He nodded. "Is there anything else? 'Cause if there's not, then I've got a couple of loose ends to hammer."

Ruben said, "Molly, please, you must help him. He is trying very hard to protect you." He took her hand in his and looked up into her eyes. "For me. For us. Tell him what you told me."

Molly sighed. "If Daddy marries Judith, he loses a major part of his land and his income from the business."

Cole raised an eyebrow. "You're not saying you think your father—"

Molly shook her head violently. "No. No, of course not." She pulled away from Ruben and crept back to her sofa. Her blue eyes filmed over and threatened to release the tears collecting at the corners of her lower lids. She blinked them back. Taking a deep breath, she said, "Judith doesn't know that he gets nothing if I'm dead, or if he remarries. Only Mother's attorney and I know."

Cole waited, hoping she would say more. When she didn't he asked, "Are you sure your father doesn't know?"

Molly blinked again. "There's no way I can be sure."

"And you think your father may be trying to kill you? What about Judith?"

Ruben said, "Mr. January, Judith Barnes may be ruthless, even unbalanced, but it's unlikely she would stoop to threats against Molly. Think of her image." He got up and paced behind the chairs, then spun around and faced Cole. "No, Mr. January, her image is far too precious to her. She has stepped on many people to get her way, but no, not threats."

Cole wasn't buying any of the information until he could check it out. Before he left, there was one other little item he had to check out, too. He pulled the folded photocopies from his pocket. "Molly, is this you on the dance floor at the Hyatt?"

She took the paper and held it in the light from the window. After several seconds she lowered it and looked up at Cole, her timidity gone, replaced by defensiveness. "What difference does it make?"

"It makes a good deal of difference," Cole said.

She flipped the paper toward him. "If you must know, it's an actress that can look enough like me that I don't have to go to those dreadful dances."

"Who is she? Where can I find her?"

Ruben said, "She's a nobody. She's not important."

Cole said, "I'll decide what's important. Answer me, Molly. Where can I find her?"

Molly dug through her purse and came up with a small address book. "I've not actually met her, and I don't know her name. Call Texas Talents. They handle her bookings."

Ruben said, "Aren't you forgetting something, Molly?"

Molly's eyes flashed sparks toward him. "It's not important now. I've told him everything."

Cole said, "I guess you didn't hear me. I get to decide what's important and what's not." He held his breath and waited for her to speak.

▽

11

MOLLY BRUSHED HER hair back from her face and gave him an apologetic half-smile. "I wasn't sure if it was important, but if you and Ruben—"

Cole said, "Spit it out."

She hesitated, then relaxed. Cole could see tension and defensiveness fade. Her voice was very calm. "Jon O'Connell was hired by my father. As a bodyguard, he's alert and has more than enough strength to physically protect me, but I've never really trusted him. Maybe it's his eyes. Or the ridiculous clothes. Or—"

Ruben said, "Come, come, Molly. Get to the point. Mr. January doesn't have all day."

Cole leaned on the back of the sofa. "You don't have to hurry on my account."

She took a deep breath. "Jon was not in his room the night that poor woman was killed. There. I've said it."

Cole couldn't have been more shocked if she had confessed to the killing herself. "Whoa! Jon may have planted that fake bomb under your car, but—did I tell you it was a fake? He's a little weird, but as far as I know he's not a killer."

Ruben said, "Then why did he lie to the police?"

"Maybe he's got a lady friend. I don't know." Cole was right about one thing—he didn't know. He didn't know the police had questioned Jon. He didn't know the police were doing anything. As much as he dreaded it, it was time for him to visit Harris. He stood up and started toward the door. "I'll check it out and get back to you."

Molly's eyes widened. "You're not going to tell Daddy anything, are you?"

"You mean like the big secret of you seeing me that you kept?" He had her pinned and let her up. He smiled and shook his head. "No, Molly, I won't say anything to your father about him or Judith or investigating Jon. But if he hired the man, I'm sure he's trustworthy. And if Judith really loves your father, she wouldn't do anything to hurt you. After all, you are still his daughter, aren't you? We'll just keep this discussion our little secret."

From somewhere, Lupe appeared and showed him to the door. She was still padding around in her bare feet, but she had added a rose to her hair. "You come back and we eat tamales and frijoles. I bery good cook."

Cole smiled at her. "Why thank you, Lupe. That sounds delicious."

She beamed and blushed across her high cheekbones. "I fix special por you, Señor."

Cole took her hand and bowed over it, leaving a light kiss on the backside. "I'd be honored to dine in your casa."

When he got in the old Chevy, he smiled to himself. He had not openly flirted with a pretty señorita since his last trip to the border, before he and Linda were married. Mexican women seemed to appreciate the game more than their northern counterparts. He had heard the rumor that in Mexico bald men were considered wealthy and intelligent until proven otherwise. He wasn't going to tell Lupe any different.

Cole was still thinking about Lupe and wondering if a fellow could get tangled up in all that hair when he pulled into the wide circle drive in front of Molly's house. Even in the shade of the big pine trees, it was hot. It was the kind of wet-sauna hot that held so much humidity there was no place for his sweat to go. The air refused to hold any more moisture. It was still and clammy. An occasional car whizzing past created the only faint, but smelly breeze.

When Jon didn't respond to the door chimes, Cole ambled

toward the garage on the west side of the house. Jon's motorcycle was there. As Cole reached for the gate to the backyard, Jon eased it open and stuck his foot against it. With a double armload of newspapers stacked above eye level, he shuffled sideways toward the garage.

Cole said, "Excuse me, Jon, but could I talk to you for a couple of minutes?"

Jon visibly flinched and turned his load of papers till he could see who was talking to him. "Oh, Mr. January. I didn't hear you come up. I have to put these in the garage, then I guess we could talk for a few minutes. I've got to go get Mr. Gomez's truck and take them to the recycle place."

Cole was only mildly disappointed that he hadn't frightened Jon enough for him to drop the papers.

Jon came back out of the garage with his hand out. "Ms. Heitkamp's not here."

Cole shook his hand. "I don't need to see her, Jon. I'd like to ask you a few questions."

Jon stepped back. "Hey, I'm sorry about last night. If I'd known it was you, I—"

"That's not why I'm here, Jon. Could we go inside? This heat is pounding on my old bald head and I just hate getting it sunburned. It bubbles up in blisters. When it peels, I look like I'm from some leper colony."

Jon looked as if it were the first time he'd noticed Cole's hair was missing. "I never thought of that. Sure."

Cole followed him through the house to his room. It was not as plush as the rest of the house, but every square foot of space was used. Cole stepped over the barbells and squeezed between the stationary bicycle and the single bed. "I understand the police questioned you."

Jon nodded as he took the other chair and turned it to fully face Cole instead of the small television set. "Yeah, the cops were okay. They wanted to know where I was the night that woman got killed. Said she looked like Ms. Heitkamp."

Cole leaned toward him. "What did you tell them?"

Jon shrugged. "Just that I was here, doing my job."

"Did anyone see you? Was Ms. Heitkamp here?"

Jon fiddled with a loose thread in the chair arm. He adjusted his position, looked at his shoes, slapped the armrest. "No, nobody saw me. I was in here. Asleep."

"Oh, come on, Jon. Is that the same lie you told the police?"

Jon jumped to his feet. "I don't have to explain anything to you. I was here. Asleep. That's all I have to say."

"Easy, Jon. What say we start over? You tell me what happened that night. Just between you and me."

Jon's eyes got almost as red as his hair. His chin quivered. He blinked, swallowed hard, and slumped back into the chair. "Please don't tell Mr. Heitkamp I wasn't here that night. He'd fire me. I know he would."

Cole raised his right hand. "I promise. Now, what say you just take your time and tell me what happened."

"My sister was in town." He paused, then hammered a fist on the armrest. "From San Antonio, see? I sneaked out after Ms. Heitkamp went to bed. I rolled my cycle out the drive without any lights and didn't start it till I was in the street." He stared at Cole, obviously wanting a comment.

Cole said, "Good thinking, Jon."

Jon nodded and tapped the side of his head. "I'm smarter than I look. I met my sister at her motel room. We talked for about two or three hours, then I came home."

Cole could see relief on the freckled face. Jon wasn't the type to hang on to a lie. "Jon, did you go anywhere else? See anyone?"

"No, sir. We stayed right there in her room. Room service brought up a pot of coffee. Maybe the guy saw me. I don't know."

Cole stood up and patted the handlebar of the stationary bike. "Looks like you've put a lot of miles on this."

Jon bobbed his carrot curls and grinned. "Yes, sir."

"Well, thanks for your time. If you think of anything else about that night, let me know."

"I will, Mr. January. Just don't tell Ms. Heitkamp I wasn't here. Her daddy would fire me for sure."

On the drive to the police station, Cole's thoughts were about as defined as a bowl of spaghetti. He couldn't tell where one thought began and another ended. He suspected Jon wasn't quite as smart as he looked, which left him not smart enough to make up the story about his sister. If that were true, that left Cole with holes in his theory that Jon was in on the murder. Maybe even innocently carried the body in or something. But if Jon wasn't involved, who was?

Cole didn't have to wait long to see Harris. The lieutenant jiggled his jowls like he was meeting an old friend. He motioned for Cole to come in and close the door while he finished what looked like turkey on pumpernickel. Around a mouthful of sandwich, Harris said, "I thought you'd be here sooner."

Cole shrugged. "I got here as fast as I could. You don't think I'd hold out on you, do you?"

"Cut the bullshit. You had the last arsonist begging to be picked up before you turned him over to us. I told you to stay out of this case. What do you know that we don't?"

Power to the powerless! Cole knew something Harris didn't and wanted to savor his discovery. He held out about as long as he could. "Just that one of the men you questioned lied like a mafia character witness."

After Harris swallowed a half-chewed bite, he bellowed, "Out with it, January! I don't have time to dance."

"Jon O'Connell was not, I repeat, not at the residence of one Molly Jones-Heitkamp on the night in question."

"So?"

"So he lied. He says he was visiting with his sister from San Antonio in her motel room."

"Very good, January. It doesn't mean shit. Did you talk to the sister? The motel clerk? Unconfirmed, all unconfirmed."

Cole watched him stuff the last of the sandwich in his mouth and pulled up a chair.

Harris drained a can of Diet Pepsi and tossed the can in a cardboard box in the corner. "Laticia saves cans for her school. Now why don't you get out of here so I can get some work done? When you've got anything I should know, come back. Or better yet, leave it alone and stay away."

Cole leaned back and stretched his legs in front of him. "I want to file a complaint."

"You know where to go. Now go!" His jowls were starting to flutter.

Cole pulled his feet in and leaned forward. "I think you may want to know about this before I go. What say I fill you in so you won't look as dumb as usual."

Harris shook his finger at Cole. "You're asking for it, January."

"Ever hear of Nathan Andrews? Or a friend of the Strangler's that goes by Hoss?"

Harris nodded.

"I figured as much. Fraizer told me he's got a list of priors."

An officer tapped on the door and opened it. "Need your signature, Lieutenant."

Harris signed the paper the officer slid onto his desk and waited for him to leave before he spoke. "What's Hoss got to do with anything?"

Cole rubbed the knot behind his ear. "I'm not sure, but I think he whacked me on the head and dumped me in my truck after I asked a few questions about the Strangler."

Harris's expression changed from stern jowl-jiggling to clenched jaw. "And you want me to bring him in?"

Cole shook his head. "Not especially. I—"

"Then get the hell out of my office!" Harris's temple twitched.

Cole stood up. "What say I come back when you're in a better mood? I don't think that sandwich agreed with you. Maybe it was the pumpernickel. Or the green turkey."

"You're the green turkey." Harris picked up a paperweight with his daughter's picture in it and drew back his arm.

Cole ducked. He didn't think Harris would throw that particular paperweight or anything else, but if he didn't duck Harris might let it fly just to keep him on his toes.

Cole threw his arms over his head. "Okay, okay. So bring in Hoss."

Harris slowly set the paperweight on a stack of files. "Can't, unless you file a complaint. He's a pet project of the mayor's. She's trying to rehabilitate him."

Cole dropped back into the chair in front of Harris. "In the words of a great man, 'So?' "

Harris hesitated. "So fill out the papers. I'd love to bring in the shithead. I'll get one of the boys on it right away." Harris almost grinned. He looked like a three-year-old going for the cookie jar. Even if he got caught, it would be worth it.

Cole said, "Will do, but there's one other little incident you might want to know about. Maybe even two. Is this a good time for you?"

"Out with it, January."

"Could have been a drunk driver, but after the roughing up I got at Judge Olsen's wingding, I don't think so."

Harris leaned back in his chair, his jowls draped into his neck. "You don't think so, what?"

"Who is James that works for Jack Heitkamp?"

Harris chanted, "Construction foreman. General flunky. Follows orders. Why?"

"He may be the man who ran me off the road just this side of Huntsville. Totaled out my truck."

"Did you get a license number?"

"I—"

Harris stood up and leaned across the desk. "Heitkamp is the only good thing about the current administration, Cole January, make no mistake. It's Heitkamp who stands up to the mayor. He makes sure the chief gets heard."

Cole opened his mouth, but was cut off.

"Who do you think talked the mayor into pushing for our last pay raise?" He sank back to the chair. "Don't go throwing mud at Heitkamp if you can't back it up."

Cole shrugged. "All I know is that Heitkamp seems to have

a lot riding on the mayor's race. He had James beat the crap out of me."

"I'll admit Heitkamp is generally a bully, but I'd be willing to also bet he thinks you're in some way a threat to his daughter." Harris picked up the paperweight and smiled at the picture. "Facts don't mean a damn when you're talking daughters."

Cole stood up and walked to the door. "Just don't come crawling to me for information. I've told you all I know."

When Harris stood up for the second time, Cole thought it was probably the most exercise the man had done all year. Harris said, "I thought you were going to leave this one alone."

"I'm not messing in your murder case, Lieutenant. I'm giving you information on my mistreatment by citizens of our fair city, totally unconnected with any murder." As Cole quickly closed the door behind him, he heard the sound but not the words Harris threw at him. It was better that way, but Cole couldn't leave it alone.

He turned the doorknob and inched the door open. A pencil bounced off the door facing and landed in the middle of the room.

"Cole! Stay away from me!"

Cole leaned his head in the partially opened door. "Anything you say, Lieutenant, but if you haven't found out who the blond bombshell in my bedroom was you might want to check with Texas Talents."

Harris jumped up from his desk and sprinted to the door. Cole heard a crash, but didn't look back.

On his way out of downtown via Smith Street and the Southwest Freeway, Cole took the exit at Kirby Drive. A quick drive-through at the Burger King and his stomach quit growling at him. It wasn't his favorite lunch spot, but they did make a decent salad to go. With HPD going after Hoss, his Luv at the mercy of his favorite claims adjuster, and some of his leads falling into place, he didn't need any help from Benny's Burritos. His brain was working on high-speed efficiency. He wouldn't have any trouble putting a name on the victim; he might have a little trouble putting a name on the killer. The one point that kept him digging wasn't to protect Molly, or even to find the murderer—it was to uncover why the body was dumped in his apartment.

Sitting in the Chevy across from the theater, Cole finished the pile of lettuce. Some days he was sure his nose would twitch like a rabbit's. As he stuffed the plastic and paper back into the bag, he glanced up in time to see Leslie pulling into a parking slot near the theater door. Cole threw the refuse on the floorboard and jumped out of the car. He was halfway across the street when he caught her eye.

Leslie stopped and waited for him. "What are you doing here, Cole? Horning in on my case?"

Cole fell in step beside her. "I could ask you the same question." He hated to admit he was glad to see her.

"Karren Janson had a part-time job here." When they reached the curb, Leslie crossed her arms and tapped her toe. "What's your excuse?"

He'd come back later to discuss Molly's stand-in if he needed to. No point in letting on to Leslie what he suspected. He matched her smug expression. "One of the actors had a spat with Molly. Henrietta quizzed him and so did I, but we both think he isn't telling everything." He crossed his arms and tapped his toe. "Satisfied?"

Leslie yanked the door open and held it back. "After you, Mr. January. Age before beauty."

Cole knew he couldn't win. If he insisted she go first, she'd accuse him of patronizing her. If he went in before her, she'd claim he had no manners. He picked the latter. "And they say chivalry is dead."

Leslie said, "If it is, you killed it." Sweeping their sparring aside, she added. "Good luck, Cole. I hope we both find what we're looking for."

Mrs. Windslow was standing on a chair, stapling another actor's picture to the wall. "We're closed. Tickets go on sale at five."

Leslie pulled a business card from her skirt pocket and held it up to her. "If you're Ms. Windslow, I think you're expecting me."

"*Mrs.* Windslow, please. My late husband— Why, Mr. January! I didn't expect to see you again." She steadied herself against the wall and dropped to the floor.

Coming at him with her hand outstretched, she was hardly recognizable to Cole. Her hair was covered by pink petals on some sort of net; she wore no makeup or jewelry. Her dark slacks and green T-shirt looked as if they'd been stolen off a teenager half her size.

Cole took her hand. "This is my associate, Leslie Commings."

Mrs. Windslow set the stapler on the desk. "I'm afraid we've told Mr. January everything we know about Molly Jones-Heitkamp, Ms. Commings."

Leslie said, "Oh, call me Leslie, and I'm not with him. I mean, I'm not working on the same case. I'm looking for a woman named Karren Janson. Texas Talents said they thought she was working for you."

"Sweet girl, that one, but not dependable. She left us without an usher last Thursday." She shook her head sadly. "I planned to use her in our next production, too."

Leslie said, "And she was here on Wednesday?"

Mrs. Windslow pulled her thin eyebrows together. "Well, yes and no. You see, she— Come back to my office. We're not likely to be interrupted there."

Leslie fell in behind her and motioned for Cole to stay back. He nodded, then cleared his throat loudly. "Mrs. Windslow, is Mr. Payne here?" If his suspicions were right, Leslie would figure out something she didn't want to know, that Molly's stand-in was Karren Janson. When she did, he hoped she was as strong as she claimed.

Mrs. Windslow motioned toward the stairs, her underarm flapping worse than the lieutenant's jowls. "Check the stage. I believe Gerald's walking through his lines."

Cole followed the directions to a door behind the staircase.

He peeked through the small diamond-shaped glass in the door. Payne shook his forefinger at an imaginary character downstage, then turned and tipped his imaginary hat at another invisible character. Cole grinned and pushed the door open.

Payne's hand flew to his chest. "Dear God, you nearly gave me a heart attack. What in heaven's name are you doing back again?"

Cole walked down the broad, shallow stairs between the seats. When he was front and center, he said, "You left out a couple of small, very small details, Payne."

Payne started to speak, but coughed several short hacks before he got any words out. "Excuse me. Nasty summer cold. I'll just get a sip of water and be right back." He sidestepped toward the curtain. "Don't go 'way."

Cole waited for several minutes, then parted the curtains. A narrow hallway circled backstage past a row of rooms before it emptied into the other side of the lobby. There were no names on the five doors along the hallway, but each was numbered. Cole supposed they were dressing rooms. He thought the lead actor should at least rate a small star. He tried the first door. It opened easily, but no one was in the room. As he stepped back into the hallway, he saw Payne dashing from Room Three.

Payne glanced over his shoulder. "I'll be right with you, Mr. January."

Cole trotted toward him. "What say I go with you?"

Payne's shoulders drooped. He stopped and faced Cole. "Very well. Just what small detail are you accusing me of hiding?"

Cole leaned against the wall, both hands in his pockets. "Remember the 'bomb'? I think you know how it got under Molly's car."

Payne sighed and rolled his eyes dramatically. "I did not have anything to do with its appearance under anyone's car. I merely loaned it to a young man for a prank."

"Jon O'Connell?"

"Why, yes. Do you know him? Quite a nice body, don't you think?"

Cole grimaced. "Now what would your friend think if he heard you talking like that?"

"He's out of town. Besides, if I ever quit looking, he may as well bury me. I'm sure I'll be quite dead."

Cole rubbed his hand back across his pate. "Would you mind telling me how you came to know Jon O'Connell?"

Payne opened the door to his dressing room and motioned Cole inside. The French decorator phone on the dresser rang a soft burr. Payne glanced at it as if it were a cockroach he hoped would return to hiding. When it rang again, he answered it and turned his back to Cole. All Cole heard was a terse "Not now."

Payne dropped the receiver in the gilded cradle. "How I know Jon is really quite simple. He was often here to pick up his sister after a performance."

"Gotcha! It couldn't have been his sister. His sister lives in San Antonio."

Payne rolled his eyes again and shook his head. "Surely one is allowed more than one sister. Anyway, we had been properly introduced, and eventually we progressed to regular visits while he waited for her. Nothing to it, really. Pity."

Cole waded through the superfluous comments and dragged the attention back to the sister. If he was ever going to confirm his suspicions, this was as good a time as any. "You mean Karren Janson, don't you?"

Payne straightened the dainty bottles on his dresser. "Yes, Karren was his sister, but when I said 'pity,' I meant that—never mind. Anyway, she didn't even stay to help clean up after the last rehearsal Wednesday. Not like her, I would think."

"Have you seen Jon since then?"

"Only when he came to pick her up that night and found she'd left. He thought she probably had a date and he'd forgotten. Some sort of miscommunication. Not at all uncommon for Jon." He turned and rested his buttocks on the dresser. "Have I been of any help, Mr. January?"

Cole reached for the door and smiled. "Yes, and I appreciate it. Break a leg."

Payne nodded. "Thanks. By the way, your body is extremely well proportioned. If you ever—"

Cole pointed a finger at the actor and erased all trace of his earlier smile. "Don't even think it, Payne."

▽

12

AS COLE CROSSED the lobby to leave the theater, Ruth Golden rushed up to him. "Why, Mr. May, so nice to see you."

Cole smiled. "You do have a way with names, don't you?"

She tapped the side of her head. "From years of memorizing lines with actors."

Cole pointed toward the door. "I was just leaving. Nice to see you, too."

Ms. Golden held up one finger. "Now I remember. You wanted some information. Right?" Without waiting for an answer, she said, "Did it have anything to do with that boy? Big fellow. Red hair. He was always hanging around while we were closing up. Seemed like a nice enough boy. Good manners and all, but that tart he picked up was too old for him."

Since Cole already knew Jon's connection with Karren, he was tempted to walk out, leaving her talking to the pictures on the wall. The last comment stopped him. "What makes you think she was a tart?"

"Oh, you know. Always changing the color of her hair. Doing something strange with her eyes. I just didn't trust her, if you know what I mean."

Cole said, "Is that all so unusual in the theater? Seems to me strange is standard stuff around here."

Ms. Golden's head bobbed affirmative. "You got that right, Mr. May—or is it March? Yes, now I remember. Definitely March." She studied her surroundings and stuck a finger to her pointed chin. "Where was I?"

"Karren."

"Oh, yes. Mrs. Windslow and I figured it out. She has some secret job that keeps her fed. We suspect it's a married lover or drug dealer. Of course, we've never thought the poor girl was using drugs."

"Is that all?"

Ms. Golden nodded. "Just that—and she never said much about herself. Most of these young people think they've had such interesting lives, they'll bend your ear six ways to Sunday if you let them. I never would sew a stitch if it was up to them."

Cole backed to the door. "If you think of anything else, let me know."

She waved cheerily and trotted toward the staircase. Cole almost doubled over with laughter when he stepped out the door. Ruth Golden did a great impersonation of Granny on "The Beverly Hillbillies," and she wasn't even trying. There were people less nuts in the nuthouse.

Thinking of nuthouses, Cole remembered he had to check out the Strangler's story. He pulled a card from his wallet and scribbled a note for Leslie. As he tucked the card under her windshield wiper, she came up behind him. "Giving me a ticket?"

Cole jumped and turned around. "You know better than to sneak up on me. What did you find out?"

"I wasn't sneaking, and I confirmed where Karren Janson worked, part-time. But Cole, I'm not any closer to where she *is*. Now I've got to find a man named Jon O'Connell. Seems he's her brother, and usually he picked her up after work."

Cole loved to watch her face when she was impressed with his talent as an investigator. He rattled off Molly's address. "You'll find your Mr. Jon O'Connell there."

She didn't disappoint him. She sighed; her eyes widened; her jaw dropped. "Man, sometimes I just don't know how you do it, but you are tops—and damn lucky."

Cole grinned on the outside, but inside he wished he could tell her the truth. It was going to hurt like hell when she found out, but if he told her, she'd claim he was giving her cases and then solving them himself. "I'd rather be lucky than good, any day of the week. Are you going back to the office first?"

Leslie opened her car door and fanned the hot air with her handbag. "Sounds like it's on the way. I'll call O'Connell from there, unless you have a better idea."

"No, just tell Henrietta I'll be in after one more stop." He stuck the card back in his wallet.

Leslie playfully grabbed his wrist. "Hey, that's my note."

Cole showed it to her. It had Jon O'Connell and Molly's address scrawled above "CJI Investigations."

Leslie smiled and impulsively kissed his cheek.

She didn't mean anything by the kiss, he told himself for the hundredth time, as he pulled into the parking lot of LeBistro. Just a friendly, appreciative gesture. His eyes adjusted to the dim lights in the lounge; his thinking adjusted to the task at hand.

For early afternoon, the lone waitress was busier than a jackrabbit in spring. Slinging drinks and sarcastic remarks, she strutted her stuff between the tables. Nobody touched her without an invitation, and it looked like open house.

Cole took a seat at one of the small tables, which couldn't hold much more than a couple of drinks and a candle. Not a wine-bottle candle like he remembered, but one of those little short, fat candles in a clear candleholder.

The waitress pranced up to him. "Okay, Slick, what'll it be?"

Cole didn't answer fast enough.

"I haven't got all day. When you figure it out, call me. Name's Maggie." She turned and twitched her tail like a bunny before she hopped to the next table.

Cole was hoping it wouldn't come to this. A friendlier, more casual conversation was more to his liking. He sighed and got to his feet. As she leaned over the table and shook her chest in front of a bleary-eyed patron who reeked of booze and money, Cole tapped her on the shoulder.

She whirled around. "You see something you want, Slick?"

Cole handed her one of his cards. "Cole January. CJI Investigations. What say you sit at my table for ten minutes."

She patted the blob. "Honey, I'll be right back."

The customer didn't have much control of his head. His nod was more of a loll that circled around and almost landed on the table. He jerked upright. "Sure, Mag."

Maggie threw one long leg across the vacant chair at Cole's table and straddled it. "Okay, Slick, what's the problem?"

"The Strangler. Last Wednesday."

Maggie tossed her long kinky hair back and turned her face to the heavens. Her position might have been inviting to the blob, but Cole considered himself a man of quality and class. If she didn't come up with some words soon, he'd track down Vicki. She couldn't be any more difficult to drag an answer from.

After two or three minutes of sitting with head back and eyes closed, Maggie sat forward. "Came in about nine-thirty with a bimbo I haven't seen before. First time he's been in here in several months. Last time was with that society bitch."

Cole was surprised at her memory and pushed it to the wall. "How many drinks did he have? What time did he leave? Did he leave alone?"

She held up one finger. "Five. Double bourbon, on the rocks." She popped up the second finger. "About midnight, give or take thirty minutes." She added the third finger. "Alone. His date left about eleven."

Cole said, "You get the silver star. What say you go for the gold? How drunk was he? Got any idea on where he went?"

"I don't play for stars, Slick Dick. Cross my palm."

Getting as far as he had without cash was more than he expected. He pulled a twenty from his wallet and slapped it on the table. He didn't pull his hand back. "Where?"

For the first time since Cole entered the lounge, Maggie smiled. "Double or nothing."

Cole, moving slower than the first time, stacked two tens on top of the twenty. "So talk."

"He was crying about the society bitch dumping him. Milly? Molly? Yeah, Molly something. Said he never had it so good. Don't know if he meant the piece of ass, the money, or the relationship. Said he was going to 'their place' so he could feel close to her, since she wouldn't see him no more. His words. My grammar is six notches above his."

Cole shoved the money toward her. "Honey, you're six notches above anything I ever saw."

She rolled the bills into a tight cylinder and slipped them in her boot. "And, Slick Dick, you ain't seen nothing yet."

Cole pushed the chair back and stood up. "What say we keep it that way."

As much as Cole knew he needed to call Henrietta, he also knew he'd best get out of LeBistro. The next invitation might be more than a man of quality and class could refuse.

When Cole reached the door, Maggie was right beside him. She danced her fingers across his head. "I just remembered another little item. I'll give it to you for free, just remember where you got it."

Cole didn't trust himself to speak. Parts of his body weren't concerned with quality and class.

"When 'I Got Friends in Low Places' came on the jukebox he yelled 'I ought to kill the bitch.' Of course, he was always yelling at the jukebox." She turned on the smile again.

Cole thanked her and left. As he was getting in the old Chevy, Maggie ran out to him. She looked better in the dim lights. "If you want to pay me for that, you can come back after midnight. We could probably work something out."

Cole pulled the door shut. He felt like a side of beef, and wondered if that was how Leslie felt when she called him a sexist. "I don't pay for volunteered info. Sorry, Tiger."

By the time Cole reached the freeway, traffic was moving at its usual standstill. He took the back roads and zigzagged toward the office. He covered more miles in less time and kept moving, too. So far, he was on schedule. He'd done everything he planned except for that one important item, which he didn't intend to leave for another day.

He opened the office door and bowed to Henrietta. Holding his eyes in a slant, he said, "Most honorable woman, be so kind to get honorable claims adjuster by way of telephone communications system. Chop-chop."

Henrietta wrinkled her nose. "If you want me to play Grasshopper, you picked a bad day."

Henrietta could go through a lot and not call it a bad day. Cole lowered his hands from his eyes and frowned. "What's the matter?"

She shrugged. "Leslie came back in tears. Now she's gone off to see Harris. Seems her missing person is your dead body."

"I know. I guess I should have told her when I first suspected it." He slid a hip on the corner of her desk. "She got any ideas why? Or who done it?"

The silence that lingered after his question was ripped by the shrill ring of the telephone. Henrietta stared at Cole and shook her head before she answered it. She nodded and made notes, but didn't say anything. Cole could hear a man's voice from where he sat.

After several minutes of listening and nodding, Henrietta said, "He's here now. You better talk to him."

She pushed the hold button. "It's Lieutenant Harris. Leslie just left there."

Cole dashed to his desk and got on the line.

Harris said, "I give up. Can we work on this together?"

Cole hesitated while he sorted out his possibilities. "Can I have Roy Fraizer and Rose Johnson?"

"Maybe."

"Have you got Hoss?"

"Maybe."

"I'm headed for Misty Glen Psychiatric Hospital. What say you send Fraizer and Johnson over to meet me. We may get this thing wrapped up before my son gets here."

Cole hung up and pointed to Henrietta. "You go home. You're going to help me pick out a truck tomorrow."

"What about Leslie? Shouldn't I be here when she gets back?"

"I'll leave her a message to meet me at Misty Glen. And don't forget to transfer the phones."

He was out the door before she could snap back. This was not exactly what he'd planned for the rest of the evening, but he hoped to trap the murderer and solve both cases before morning. That would give him plenty of time to get ready for Kevin's visit. He felt bad about the way he had shortchanged his preparations. He didn't even have tickets to the Astros-Dodgers game yet.

On the way to Misty Glen, Cole started stirring all the pieces together. It was speculation, but he could see how it was possible. The Strangler did it; Hoss covered for him. Hoss got scared when he showed up at the gym and knocked him out as a warning to stay away. Jon's sister was dead because the Strangler was too drunk to tell the difference. That left the beating he took and getting his truck run off the road. If Harris was right, those could result from Heitkamp's nutty idea that he was a threat to Molly. The only stink in the stew was where the body was found.

At this point, he could easily accept a warped version of Jennifer Ann's theory—it could be as simple as he forgot to lock his door. Like the mountain climber's reason for the climb—it was there. Maybe he was closer to the top of the mountain than he thought.

Feeling the power of conquest, Cole approached the receptionist at the front desk of Misty Glen. She looked up at him and smiled. "Let me guess. You want to see our favorite wrestler."

A confession of his identity would spoil her day, he decided. He pointed a finger at her bright eyes and drawled, "Good memory, ma'am."

By the time he reached Jimmy's room, apprehension had eroded his confidence. If Jimmy didn't do it, he was back to go. He'd have to hold on to his theory and fight to expose Jimmy.

He tapped lightly on the door and pushed it open. When he saw the Strangler, he knew it would be a lopsided match at best.

Jimmy looked as if he were ready to turn himself in to anyone who would take him. Cole thought he must have stayed awake all night to get such dark circles under his eyes. He was sitting in the middle of the unmade bed, hugging a pillow, and barely acknowledged Cole.

Cole whispered, "Mind if I come in?"

Jimmy seemed to focus on the mirror to Cole's left. "Does it make any difference?"

Cole closed the door behind him. "Probably not."

Looking less like the Strangler than Tinkerbell, Jimmy eased his legs off the bed. "I had a feelin' you'd be back." He hung his head and stared at the floor.

"Just hoping your brain is defogged enough for you to remember last Wednesday night," Cole said. "If you still don't know, maybe I can jog your memory."

Jimmy's head snapped up. What might have passed for hope sprang to his eyes. "What'd you get? Did Vicki know?"

Cole shook his head. "Maggie. She said you yelled that you ought to kill the bitch. Remember that?"

"Aw, no, man. I wouldn't say that. No way." He scrambled off the bed and backed to the far wall.

"Why'd you do it, Jimmy? Couldn't stand being dumped?"

Jimmy collapsed on the floor under the window. The beefy muscles on his heavy frame drooped like last week's daylily. The sparrows at the birdbath fluttered their wings and splashed in the water. Cole couldn't hear the birds, and he couldn't hear what Jimmy was thinking. "Talk to me, Jimmy. Why did you do it? Why did you put her in my room?"

With both hands, Jimmy pulled his head between his knees and moaned, then he pounded the wall with his fist. "No! No! No! I didn't kill nobody!"

He jumped to his feet and came at Cole. Cole quickly learned how Jimmy got his ring name.

Suddenly, the room was full of people: Two orderlies and

a nurse in white and Fraizer in the worst-looking tie Cole had ever seen. Fraizer never looked more fashionable.

The orderlies grabbed Jimmy from each side and squeezed him between them. They were each almost as big as the sergeant. Fraizer slowly walked behind them and clicked on the bracelets. As the orderlies relaxed their grip, Fraizer said, "Read it, Rosie."

Cole grinned. If there was anything Rose Johnson hated, it was to be called Rosie. She stepped into the room and shot Fraizer a death-wish look. She read the patient his rights in a seething monotone.

When she finished reciting, Cole rubbed his throat and said, "I'll see you at the station. I'm hoping Harris will let me question Hoss."

Jimmy jerked at the handcuffs like a chained Doberman. "Ha! You won't get anywhere with him. He's the mayor's pretty boy."

Cole stepped up to him. "He's anything but pretty, hasn't been a boy in a bunch of years, and he's already bragged about knocking me out. I'd have to say he's dumb, too."

The nurse cleared her throat. "I'll have to see something official before I can let you take this patient out of here."

Cole turned to her. "He's in here on a voluntary, isn't he?"

She nodded.

"Then he's coming with us—voluntarily."

Jimmy threw back his head and yelled. It was an ear-piercing, heart-stopping yell carried by a whole lungful of air. When he stopped, he looked up at Fraizer. "I demand to see my lawyer."

Rose punched her finger against his chest in rhythm with her words. "Listen to me, you frog-faced hulk, you'll get your phone call at the police station. If I hear one more rebel yell out of you, you won't have any lips to talk with when you make that phone call. You got that?"

As they marched down the hall with Rose and Fraizer on each side of Jimmy and the nurse leading the way, Cole heard

Leslie in the lobby. "But I know he's here working on a case. He told me to meet him here."

Cole came up behind her and winked at the receptionist. "Sorry, ma'am. She thinks I'm a private detective. Ridiculous, isn't it? We'll come back tomorrow when the doctor's in."

Leslie whirled around. She boxed him on the biceps. "I could kill you, Cole January."

"Can I quote you on that?" Maybe the quick comeback would get her to lighten up. Henrietta hadn't exaggerated. Leslie had been crying for a long time. Her eyes were swollen and, in spite of fresh makeup, still red-rimmed. It looked like she was going to take special handling.

Cole put his arm around her shoulders and guided her toward the door. "What say I buy you dinner after we finish up at the station?"

"Do I get to decide where?"

"Maybe."

▽

13

COLE PARKED ON the south side of the city jail on Reisner Street and dug out the quarters in his console. He thought Leslie was right behind him, but realized she must have pulled into one of the metered slots on the far side of the paved lot. Waiting near the curb, he watched her come toward him. He knew he should have more urgent matters on his mind, but it was the first time he'd noticed she'd lost her country swagger. She walked smoothly, as if she were gliding over the uneven pavement.

When she first came to work for him she'd stomped around like a cowboy fresh from two weeks in the saddle. When he'd watched her learning to walk in high heels, it was torture to look at her. He was sure she would fall over and break something before she got the hang of it.

Cole couldn't take his eyes off her. He didn't understand why they fought, or why she suddenly looked so good. Since his divorce he'd been very cautious. He flirted with all the women, admired many, and dated only a few. He liked to think of himself as a confirmed bachelor with a burst of temporary insanity that had lasted a few months shy of nine years. He didn't plan to let that happen again.

As Leslie walked up to him, she looked worried. "Did you have your radio on?"

"I don't even know if the old crate has a radio. Why?"

"The guy on the news said somebody shot at Judith. You reckon— Do you suppose there's some lunatic out there trying to kill off both sides of the mayor's race?"

Cole grinned. "Yeah, I reckon." He didn't think this was the time to tell her he'd seen Judith. He still hadn't verified that she'd been out of town on Wednesday. Just because someone fired through her window didn't mean they were after her in particular. Random drive-by shootings were not uncommon in Houston. True, they usually happened in other parts of town, but it was too common to guarantee it was someone out to kill Judith. A gang of kids with a stolen gun may have been aiming for her cockatoo.

Cole wasn't sure how his thoughts had wandered so far from the woman beside him. Sometimes it seemed his mind had a mind of its own, so to speak. He looked down at their feet as they crossed Reisner Street, walking in step, silent.

At the top of the wide stairs, Cole held the heavy door open without thinking. Leslie mumbled a thank-you and didn't seem to mind. The elevators were operating more slowly than usual, but they finally reached their destination. Cole and Leslie stepped out and marched down the hall.

From a doorway, Fraizer waved them back to the interrogation room, where Jimmy and Rose stared at each other across a metal table.

Rose looked up as Cole and Leslie entered. "Looks like you got your man, Cole, but nobody can prove it. Anything you want to ask him?"

Cole looked down at the Strangler. He could feel disgust churning his stomach. "Anybody that would kill a beautiful woman can't be much of a man."

Jimmy jumped to his feet and opened his mouth. Fraizer shoved him down before he could speak.

Fraizer said, "We don't have much to go on, but he's got no alibi and lots of motive."

Rose said, "I understand Jon-Boy wasn't nighty-night like he told us, either."

Cole nodded. "But I got the same info from the motel's night clerk that you did. As long as we can't pinpoint the time he arrived and departed, we don't have anything on Jon either way. Where's Hoss?"

Fraizer motioned over his shoulder toward the general direction of the cells. "In the holding tank."

Leslie walked up to the table. "Did you know her real name was Janice Phillips? Did you know she had a cat? A family?"

Jimmy held his head in his hands and rocked from side to side. "I swear by all that's holy, I don't know nothing about none of this. I don't know nobody named Janice Phillips. I wouldn't hurt her if I did."

Cole slapped the table. "How 'bout Karren Janson?"

Jimmy shook his head violently and pounded the table. "Man, I don't fucking know what you're talking about!"

Rose said, "You still want your lips or you want me to rip 'em off?"

Jimmy put his hands in his lap and sat up straight. "I want to talk to my lawyer."

Fraizer said, "Hacksaw's trying to find him."

"Then I want to talk to Hacksaw."

Cole said, "So do I."

Rose pushed her chair back and stood up. "We haven't got enough to book him, Cole. You want us to hold him overnight or let him go back under his rock?"

"Turn him loose."

Hoss wouldn't talk. Cole swore he'd make the assault charge stick if he had to take it to the Supreme Court. Hoss still wouldn't talk.

Cole said, "The mayor's gonna be downright nasty when you get yourself convicted."

Hoss said, "Fuck the mayor. She can't touch me."

One more time Cole asked, "Why did you tell Sergeant Fraizer you knocked me out and dumped me in my truck?"

One more time, Hoss said, "You've lost it, January. You ought to be at Misty. I never said I did anything to you."

Hoss held up until Cole was too hungry and tired to care whether he knew anything about Jimmy killing the woman. He didn't even care if Hoss had whacked him on the head.

Since there was no way to prove or disprove it and Leslie looked exhausted, Cole motioned to the officer standing by. "Take him away. We're leaving."

Leslie followed Cole back to the elevators. "I'll take a rain check on the dinner, Cole. I want to go to the motel and talk to Darcy."

Cole held the elevator door open. "Then I'll go with you. We can eat later."

Leslie didn't speak again until they were on the steps in front of the station. She stopped about halfway down and turned to face him. "Are you going so you can keep me company or to see if I can handle it?"

Cole threw up his hands. "For Pete's sake, woman, what is this? The Inquisition? Forget it." He picked up his pace and crossed Reisner Street before she reached the corner.

Driving slowly and aimlessly, delving into his conversations with Leslie in the recent past, he still had no clue as to what motivated her. Was she looking for a bigger office or trying to get booted out so she could start her own agency and blame him when it failed? It wasn't unusual for a junior partner to sprout wings for a solo flight.

As Cole pulled off the street, he realized he was rolling into the parking lot at Benny's Burritos. He decided to skip the chili—nothing could help him understand women—and grab a taco salad. He could still make it to Molly's before dark.

Benny's Burritos was one of those places that looked the same as it did in the fifties when Benny was a boy. Mexican serapes, sombreros, and embroidered dresses decorated the wall above brightly painted, straw-seated chairs and economy-sized tables. The only addition to the decor since the place opened was a bullfight poster dated 1963, which Benny had brought back, along with a bride, from one of his trips south. Cole suspected it was an arranged marriage. Benny seemed to get more enjoyment from the poster than the wife.

After Cole polished off the cheese, meat, tomatoes, and onions on top, he chewed his way through the lettuce to the bottom of the bowl-shaped taco shell. He wiped his face, wadded the napkin, and stood up—nose to nose with Leslie.

Cole didn't say anything; he didn't know what to say. He drank the last of his tea and set the large paper cup back on the table.

Leslie's eyes looked worse than they had at the hospital. "Cole, it was awful."

She sounded like a little girl. He wanted to take her in his arms and kiss away her tears. "I should have gone with you. It's tough on anybody to tell a client their search ended with a body. Was Jon there?"

She bit her quivering lower lip and nodded. "The police had already contacted them."

"They identified their sister?"

She nodded again and threw herself in one of the chairs. "I feel like I lost a friend I never got to meet."

Cole said, "I know. It's happened to me once with a runaway. The poor kid had tried to ride the rails and didn't make it. It hurts like hell." It was one of those cases he tried not to think about. He held out his hand to her. "Come on, Les. What say we go somewhere and have a drink?"

She got up and followed him to the parking lot. "Not tonight. I've gotta find a place for a homeless kitty."

Cole walked her to her car, then leaned into the window while she fished her keys from her purse. He didn't want to push, but her hands were shaking, and she didn't sound as if she should be alone. "The cat will be okay. What say we worry about Fluffy tomorrow? Want to buy me a drink?"

She sighed. "Oh, Cole, you're hopeless. Okay. Where?"

"I know just the place. Follow me."

Maggie kissed Cole's bald head and left bright red lip prints. "What'll it be, Slick Dick?"

After Maggie took their order and left, Leslie said, "Charming. A friend of yours?"

Cole took her hand in both of his. "No, but you are. I wish I could make this easier for you."

"And I wish I'd stayed in Cedarbrake. I've tried to remember why I came to the big city, and none of it seems important now."

Even in the dim light, Cole could see her eyes clouding up again. "It's important to me that you came to Houston. You could have gone to Dallas, and look what I'd have missed. You're a good investigator. Look how quick you solved that medical insurance fraud case."

She smiled weakly. "Thanks, but you don't have to coddle me. I won't break."

He stared into her shimmering eyes. "I don't coddle."

When she started to speak, Cole went with his impulse. He gently placed a hand behind her head and pulled her toward him. Their lips met briefly before she got her hand on his shoulder and pushed. "Cole. Don't. You don't have to—"

Cole whispered, "I know."

This time he felt her hand pull. Mixing business and pleasure never seemed so right.

Cole leaned back and smiled at her. She looked softer, more vulnerable than a homeless kitten. He didn't even look up when Maggie sat their drinks on the table. It had been a long time since he had let himself feel tender toward a woman. He lifted his drink. "To the future."

Maggie tapped his shoulder. "If you don't pay me, you won't have a future." She twitched her tail. "Unless you want to run a tab?"

Leslie reached for her handbag.

Cole handed Maggie his plastic. "No tab. We've gotta go check on a kitty."

He flipped on the lights as they entered his apartment. "I've got some white wine in the fridge. Sound good?"

Leslie squatted to pet Fluffy. "Doesn't white go with chicken? It ought to suit me tonight. I don't feel very brave."

Cole pulled her up and held her. It was long past dark. Molly would have to wait till morning. "You've had a hard day, Leslie, and I don't want to make it any harder for you."

She leaned her head on his shoulder. "You've taken good care of me, but—"

"The cat can stay here another day. Do you want to go home?"

Leslie pulled back from him. "Not unless you want me to, but—"

Brushing her hair back from the side of her face, he said, "But what?"

"But I'm so hungry I could eat your darn goldfish."

"Blondie? Not a chance. Besides, Fluffy got first dibs. You'll have to settle for pretzels and cheese." He pulled a box from the pantry and shook it. "Or Mellow Crunch, the breakfast of underdogs."

If he kept it light, Cole hoped to avoid one of those awkward situations where he didn't know what to say next. Their eyes locked. It was too late. He had to pick her up and carry her to the bed—or send her home.

Jerking his gaze back to the cereal box, he set the food on the counter, then took his only two wineglasses from the cabinet. He grinned. "A bag of pretzels, a glass of wine, and thou?"

Leslie slowly took off each earring as she talked. "You sweet talker, you. Will Henrietta ever forgive us for taking away her referee job?"

Cole filled the glasses and passed one to her. "Probably not, but ask me if I care."

Leslie drew her finger across his bottom lip, then kissed it. It wasn't awkward anymore.

The morning sun sneaked in through the one bent slat in the miniblinds. Cole rose up on one elbow and ran his finger along the thin ribbon of light draped across Leslie's bare hip. As she stirred and stretched, the twisted sheet slipped off her breasts. Cole leaned down and kissed the tip of each one.

She squeezed his head against her chest, then pulled him up by his ears. She opened her eyes and looked at him. "It wasn't a dream, was it?"

Cole nuzzled her neck. "And it wasn't a nightmare, either, I trust."

Leslie scrambled to a sitting position and pulled the sheet up around her. "Oh, Cole, I know how you feel about mixing business and . . . I didn't mean to . . . Cole, you're not . . ."

Cole chuckled. "I can't very well fire the best partner I ever had—in or out of bed."

Leslie grinned. "You weren't bad for an old man."

He pounced on her and wrestled the sheet from between them. "I'll show you who's old!"

It took him a while to show her, but she didn't seem to mind. When the ringing phone clicked over to the answering machine downstairs, Cole never heard it.

By the time they finally made it down to the kitchen, Leslie said, "I don't think I can handle pretzels and cheese for breakfast. Got any milk for that Mellow Crunch?"

Cole pushed the rewind button before he answered. "No, but it's not bad by the handful."

The machine whirred and clicked. "Cole, this is Molly. I need to talk to you. I know it's early, but—just get over here as soon as you can."

It wasn't exactly what Cole had in mind, but he didn't have any choice. Either he kept the client happy, or he didn't get paid. He didn't think one less spoiled, rich blond in the country would be any great loss. He also didn't object to taking her money.

He had thought she was stronger, smarter, different—but even frightened, she was demanding. She also had lousy timing. He would earn every nickel he collected.

Leslie came up behind him and put her arms around him. She snuggled her head against his back. "Want me to go with you?"

Cole swiveled in her arms and held her chin in his hand. "Are you offering to go with me because you don't think I can handle it?"

"Never let a gal up, do you?"

He kissed her nose. "Not if I don't have to, but since

Henrietta's expecting one of us to show up for work, you're elected. She was almost as worried about you as I was."

"Can I tell her we've signed a peace treaty?"

"She won't believe you."

While they were dressing, Leslie said, "Cole, do you think Janice was killed because she looked like Molly, or was it over the inheritance?"

"What inheritance?"

Leslie looked wide-eyed. "Gosh, Cole, didn't I tell you? That's why her sister was looking for her. Their grandmother died and left them a bundle."

"A bundle? As in cash?"

"I think Darcy said it was in a trust. If they couldn't find her, the court has to appoint an attorney ad litem to represent her interest. That would cost the estate, and leave less for Darcy and Jon."

Cole's thoughts raced ahead of her. And if there wasn't a second sister, there'd be more for them to divide. Jon didn't seem that money-hungry, but he hadn't met Darcy. If there really was a big estate, she may have— He threw on the brakes of his runaway mind. "I'll meet you at the office. Stay there. I want you with me when I go see Darcy."

Leslie held her lipstick in front of her. "But, Cole, if Darcy and Jon had anything to do with Janice's murder, why would they put her in your apartment?"

Cole rubbed his hair in place. "How the hell do I know? I'll be there as soon as I finish with Molly."

Leslie ran her fingers through her short hair and smoothed her skirt. "Whatever Molly wants, Molly gets. Is that it?"

Cole tucked in his shirt. "Something like that, but she'll never make partner in my company."

She swatted his butt. "Get out of here."

▽

14

COLE STEPPED INTO the foyer and closed the door. The words slipped out before he had time to think. "You look like hell."

Molly had on a dark-green terry-cloth robe. It covered everything between her bare legs and deep cleavage. She might have looked sexy if her hair wasn't sticking up in limp spikes between rats' nests. It would help if she'd washed off the mascara smeared under her eyes like lampblack on a pass receiver.

She pulled the robe together around her neck. "Thanks, but I'm not sure how to dress when my life is in danger, Mr. January."

The sarcasm was a new twist. Cole thought it was a healthy sign, and typical of the species. He followed her across the thick carpet to the brocade sofa. "Want to tell me why you look like the debutante from hell?"

Molly turned and stared at him as if she didn't quite understand what he said. She rubbed the back of her hand across her cheek and smeared away a dark streak. "If you must know, Ruben just left."

Cole was sorry he asked. He didn't blush, but he did feel he'd overstepped a boundary. He squirmed and adjusted his position on the sofa. Pulling the small notepad from his hip pocket, he said, "What say you start with telling me what prompted this call."

"Which you did not bother to return." She seated herself across from him. Curling her legs under her, she took a deep breath and let it out slowly. "I think you should know where I was the night of the murder. Cole, it's all coming to a head. The media is going to pounce on it, and I'm going to help them."

Cole leaned forward. "You said you were here. How else could you know Jon wasn't here?"

Her exasperated sigh emptied her lungs. "Because I went to his room when I got in. I wanted him to be prepared."

"For what?" Molly's twisted sense of honesty had him completely puzzled.

"This isn't easy, Cole, so listen closely. I've found enough evidence to have Jack at least investigated and possibly convicted, along with several other city officials." She leaned back and smiled. "When the news breaks, Ruben will be the only decent choice the voters have."

Cole stood up and walked to the window. Did Jack Heitkamp suspect him of helping Molly dig up the dirt that would ruin him? It would certainly explain the beating. "Does he know what you've got?"

She shook her head. "He might know someone has been through his files, but I doubt he suspects it was me. That's what I was doing that night. When I found what I was looking for I called Ruben, and we met with the key people on our campaign staff."

Cole whirled around. "I know you weren't at the theater for dress rehearsal. Did anyone else know you weren't there?"

"Just the people at Texas Talents, the actress they sent over, and that actor, Gerald Payne. I think that's his name."

That was a bit of flavoring he'd left out of his stew. Good old Pain-in-the-ass Gerald. He'd have to give that more thought later. It was the political pie he was cutting into now. "Did anyone on Townsend's staff know you weren't at the theater?"

Molly shook her head. "In a clandestine operation, one seldom announces one's actions to the opposition."

Cole grabbed her shoulders and leaned into her face. "Why did Gerald Payne know the difference?"

Molly's eyes widened. "He was her acting coach. He was very impatient with her. She had trouble remembering to keep her lips closed when she smiled. That is one of the reasons I had him on the list in the first place. That and"—she paused—"and his unreasonable temper."

Cole said, "He told me you two had an argument, but it sounded tame to me."

"That's because he told it. He threatened to kill me if I didn't arrange to have him nominated for the Esther Philmore Grant for the Performing Arts that Mother endowed. He damn well knows that anyone nominated by me and the mayor will be the recipient."

Cole backed to the sofa and dropped onto it. "And if Ruben wins, you'd be in a position to see that he gets that nomination. So it wouldn't make sense for him to be angry enough to want you dead."

Molly looked down at her hands folded in her lap before she spoke. "When I refused to even consider mentioning his name, he said I'd recommend him or I'd damn well wish I had."

Cole leaned forward, his elbows resting on his knees. "And what about Judith Barnes? Remember, she's been shot at. Do you think it had anything to do with the attempts and threats on your life?"

Molly stood up abruptly. "I'm going to change into something more appropriate for this quiz show. Can I get you a drink?"

Cole shook his head. "I'm fine, but you go ahead. I'll wait. I've just got a few more points I want to cover. Do you mind if I use your phone?"

After she pointed toward the library, he watched her clutch the robe at the top with one hand and tug the hem down behind her with the other as she minced her way across the thick mauve carpet and down the hallway. When she was out of sight, he stepped across the foyer to the library.

Cole didn't miss her sudden changing of the subject. It was so blatant that he wondered if he was putting too much emphasis on it. Maybe she only wanted to get dressed. Sure. And maybe the rest of the summer was only going to be slightly warm.

While he waited for Henrietta to answer, he wondered if Molly would tell him what she thought might connect her danger with Judith being shot at. Maybe it was his imagination, but it looked to him as if Molly was playing both sides against him. If Daddy Jack was involved in criminal activities, would she turn him in or settle for using the knowledge to get Gomez elected? Or some other unnamed favor?

Henrietta had a smile in her voice when she answered. Cole said, "This must be a better day." A better day for Henrietta did not necessarily mean a better day in general. If anything, her up mood made him cautious. "Anything going on that I need to know about?"

"Leslie just told me you said I could have that poor homeless kitty."

He hadn't said that, but he was glad Leslie had thought of it and given him credit. "If that makes you happy, maybe I ought to check you in at Misty Glen."

In a voice that would have made Zsa Zsa proud, Henrietta said, "Dahling, you must be joking. Hanging around zat place could ruin my reputation."

When she was satisfied with Cole's laugh, she cleared her throat and shifted to her efficient-secretary voice. "Two calls. The receptionist at Misty Glen said your question on the stereo was referred to Housekeeping. Housekeeping claims it was brought in the day after Jimmy checked in. Not standard. Has not been removed.

"Second call. Judith Barnes. Wants to talk to you about finding the gunman who shot at her through her living room window. She sounded like she should take a long trip to Misty Glen without a stereo."

Cole wrote down Judith's number. "Is Leslie there?"

Henrietta scraped her fingernails across the receiver. "Static on the line, Sergeant. Do you copy?"

"Broderick, this is Jack." He paused and dropped his

voice to a deep monotone. "All I want is the facts, ma'am. Is Private Investigator Leslie Commings on the scene?"

Leslie said, "Not bad, but there's still a touch of Texas in your voice."

Cole chuckled and felt his face redden. It wasn't that she hadn't heard him play movie voices with Henrietta before, but she'd caught him off guard. Surprised him. He felt silly and defensive at the same time. He said, "You got any objection to Texas?"

"Not even a teensy bit. What can I do for you?"

Cole had several ideas, but said, "Call Harris and tell him I need Fraizer and Johnson. I'll check back to confirm."

"I can do that. Anything else?"

Cole had a hunch his next request was unnecessary, but just to be sure, he said, "They finally booked him. Find out who, if anyone, went the bail for Hoss."

He guessed from the long pause that Leslie was writing everything down. He waited for her okay, then said, "Meet me at Mid-Town Gym in about an hour. Bring Henrietta. Tell her to transfer the phones and close the office. This is important."

Leslie's voice was very grave. The lady knew when to take him seriously. "You can count on us, Cole."

Cole heard Molly's sandals clack on the floor behind him. He mumbled a quick good-bye and hung up.

Molly looked like a different woman. Her blond hair was all feathered curls and wispy bangs. The gauzy blouse and silk shorts she wore covered less than the terry robe, but she wasn't tugging at anything. She smiled. "Better?"

Cole raised an eyebrow. "Definitely. What say we get back to business?"

"I'm meeting Ruben at the country club when we're finished here. After the tennis match this afternoon, we're having dinner. I don't suppose you'd care to join us?"

Curious though Cole was about the elaborate country club that served the area's idle rich, he declined. "I only need a couple of answers, and you can be on your way."

Molly sat in the padded swivel chair behind the rolltop desk and motioned to the ladder-back chair beside it. "I thought about what you asked about Judith. All I can say is it could be, but I don't know. I can't believe any of this is happening."

Cole tipped the chair back on two legs. "Are you serious about exposing your father?"

Molly said, "First of all, he's a stepfather. Actually, he adopted me when I was very young, but I'm not a biological daughter and never want to be. He did nothing but take advantage of Mother and me."

"Is that a yes?"

Molly nodded slowly, her teeth clamped, her jaw tight. "I intend to see him get everything he deserves. In a very few years I'll be thirty. If I don't get the truth out by then, he'll be in a position to gain access to the estate Mother left me. All he has to do is prove me incapable of managing my own affairs, and he can get a guardianship"—she snapped her fingers—"that quick."

Cole felt his jaw go slack and thought he probably looked like an idiot. "You? Incapable? Seems to me that wouldn't exactly be easy to prove."

Molly slapped her palm on the desk. "You have no idea how difficult it is to stop him. He is a very determined and very ingenious barracuda of a man."

She motioned for Cole to step behind the desk. From the front, he hadn't realized she had a stack of paper from a computer printout. She indicated the headings, then the bottom lines.

Cole wasn't a bookkeeper by anyone's standards. Henrietta kept his checkbook. Still, he could tell she had a clear case of "Jack stuck in his thumb and pulled out a plum." Nobody was going to tell him he was a good boy.

When Cole left Molly's, he believed her. If Jack Heitkamp wanted to discredit her, he would find a way—just like he found a way to stay rich. Even without her claim that someone was trying to kill her, he could have her committed for seventy-two hours. During that time, Jack might convince the evaluating psychiatrist that her accusation that he was after her money was all a figment of her imagination. Cole did realize that there may or may not be someone trying to kill Molly. A fake bomb or a note put together from magazine clippings could be produced by anyone: a stepfather, adopted father, bodyguard, killer—or Molly herself.

It seemed the more Cole realized, the less he knew. He did know there *had* been a murder and the body *was* found in his bedroom. If the police were any closer to finding the murderer than he was, they weren't telling.

Cole saw Leslie's car parked in the handicapped slot in front of Mid-Town Gym and Training Club. Henrietta's portable sign graced the back window. When he pulled into the slot beside it and turned off the ignition, the old Chevy dieseled to a shuddering stop. He didn't know what the usual procedure was, but Hacksaw's brother-in-law could tow the blue bomb to wherever they wanted it. He had driven it as far as he was going to.

Henrietta waved at him from the lat-builder machine. Her hands gripped the pull-bar, her grin as big and bright as Hacksaw's. He was standing beside her, showing her how to use the mechanical contraption to increase her arm strength. Leslie was leaning on the counter, idly spinning her keys on the slick Formica, a dreamy and patient expression on her face.

Cole put his hand on her shoulder. "What say we blow this joint."

Leslie looked back at him and grimaced. "Cole, nobody has said 'blow this joint' in at least twenty years. Maybe thirty."

Cole shrugged. "So I'm out of date. Want to trade me in on a younger model?"

She turned to face him and slid her arms around his neck. "Not a chance."

"Then let's get Ms. Bodybuilder out of here and . . . hit the trail? Get the show on the road? Split?"

Leslie giggled. "How 'bout if we get Henrietta and just leave?"

"Great idea!"

By the time they pulled into A. J. Wilson's Chevrolet "Salearama" auto lot, Cole had heard all the discussion on new cars he never wanted to hear. Henrietta wanted him to get a big luxury sedan; Leslie wanted him to go for a four-wheel-drive all-terrain vehicle.

From the backseat Cole said, "Ladies! I want your input. Really. But let's see what they've got that I can afford. Okay?"

Leslie slouched down low behind the wheel. "I'm from a serious truck-buying family. Hope nobody sees us looking at sissy trucks or toy cars."

Henrietta touched Leslie's shoulder. "Hey, he's out of that ancient sissy truck. There's hope."

In spite of Cole's desire to get this decision out of the way, there was more to selecting a new vehicle than he remembered. The glass-enclosed showroom displayed the top of the line in pickups and sedans. A van complete with fold-down bed was tempting. Out on the lot, there were more choices. The salesman took them past the body shop to the truck lot. Cole stopped at a red Silverado with a supercab.

Henrietta pounded her fist against the rear tire. "I think it's tough enough for you. And it's red. That ought to cinch it."

Leslie's gaze swept the truck from bumper to bumper. "It may be more truck than you can handle, Cole. I'd hate to see you get in over your head. I mean, it's got the supercab and the whole enchilada."

The salesman clicked his ballpoint and scratched numbers on the back of his business card. He held it up to Cole. "I can let you have it for this little price right here."

Cole's breath came out in a whistle. He staggered and clutched his chest. "Ladies, we have to look elsewhere. A rich man, I'm not."

They went to the Dodge dealer and checked out a Ram, then to the Jeep dealer to look over a Cherokee, before they went to John Luke Ford. Henrietta elected to wait in the cool showroom while Cole and Leslie followed the salesman in white shoes to the row of F-150s.

Leslie whispered, "Just don't get a green one. Somebody I know has one, but I can't remember who. Besides, red is the real you."

Cole nodded and caught up with the salesman. "Say, do you do much bodywork here?"

The salesman flashed a practiced smile. "We sure do. Got one of the best paint-and-body outfits in the city. His smile vanished. "You're not planning on wrecking it right away, are you?"

Cole smiled. "Can't be too prepared these days."

The hot sun had Cole's head sweating, and he knew Leslie would be willing to go anywhere cool. He had found everything he was looking for. He shook hands with the salesman. "Thanks for your time. We'll let you know when we decide."

As they walked back to the showroom to get Henrietta, Leslie leaned toward Cole. "What happened? I thought you were ready to buy a truck and all of a sudden we're leaving."

Cole winked at her. "We've got places to go and things to do, Leslie, my lady love."

▽

15

COLE CALLED FROM the pay phone at the Texaco across the freeway. They could have it ready by six, the man said. He sauntered back to the car and crawled into the backseat. "You ladies hungry? What say we grab a drive-through, my treat, and head for the office?"

Leslie turned around and stared at him. "Well?"

Looking as innocent as Fluffy sitting beside Blondie's tank, Cole shrugged. "What?"

She huffed and threw the car in gear.

Henrietta said, "There's a drive-through if you stay on the feeder."

Chicken-stuffed pita tacos from the Jack-in-the-Box added a new aroma to Leslie's car and decorated its cloth upholstery with shredded lettuce. She fussed at her sloppy passengers, but Cole noticed that she dropped her fair share.

By the time they reached the office, his two pita tacos were gone and so was his hunger. He jumped out of the car and helped Henrietta with her chair in spite of her protests.

After she lowered herself into the chair, she put a spin on one wheel while holding the other stable and did a one-eighty away from the car. "I manage every morning without your help, Coleman, and I'll thank you kindly to keep your mitts off me. Just hand me my window sign."

"My, my. A bit touchy, aren't we?"

"The first weekday I've been anywhere, and you don't even tell me which vehicle you've decided on." She raised her fist toward him. "One of these days . . . one of these days"—she smacked her fist into her other palm—"Pow! Right in the kisser!"

Cole grinned. She needed a lot of work on that one, but she had the emphasis right. He pointed at her. "Jackie Gleason."

"Get out of here."

He unlocked the office door, then went back to the car. Just before Henrietta pulled the door shut he shouted, "The Silverado!"

He slid into the passenger seat and leaned back with his hands behind his head. "I could get used to having a chauffeur. Drive on, Jeeves."

"The name's still Leslie Commings. You keep talking like that and you'll be walking."

Cole lowered his hands.

She flashed a forgiving grin at him. "Where are we going, Lord January?"

Her British accent was better than his, but not up to Henrietta's. "To that infamous one-star motel. We've got business with Sister Darcy and Brother Jon."

The motel faced the Southwest Freeway. Road construction blocked the main entrance off the freeway feeder road. Leslie turned up the narrow street that bordered the south side of the three-story building, then wound her way through the parking lot. Cole spotted Jon's motorcycle on the tail rack of a car several slots over from where she parked.

When Cole tapped on the door, the sound interrupted the voices inside.

Jon yelled. "Just a minute!"

In less than minute, Jon opened the door. "Oh, Mr. January. I'm surprised to see you here."

"I'll just bet you are."

The unmade double bed was topped by the open suitcase Darcy was packing. The cheap print over the bed was secured to the wall. The plastic-coated dresser left only a narrow trail between it and the foot of the bed. Except for the window, beige drapes drawn, the other walls were interrupted only by the closet door and the bathroom door. Both doors were open.

Jon, in jeans and a Just-Do-It shirt instead of one of his bizarre costumes, held an open hanging bag. He zipped it closed and hung it on the bathroom doorknob.

Cole asked, "Going somewhere?"

Darcy's eyes were swollen and red. She dabbed at her nose with a tissue. "I've got to get home and make the arrangements."

Jon said, "I can't believe anyone would kill her, Mr. January. Have you found out anything about who did it? Or why?"

Cole waved for Leslie to join him and stepped inside. When Leslie entered the room, Cole said, "I'm fairly sure who killed your sister and why, but I need to know a few facts from the two of you."

Darcy nodded. "Anything we can do to help." She blotted her eyes. "God, what a waste. She was so young. So pretty. I . . ."

Leslie put her arm around Darcy's shoulders. "I know it's hard, and this is a bad time to try to think, but Cole needs your help."

Cole thought Leslie handled that very well. Everyone likes to think they're helping, especially if the one they're helping is purported to be an expert. The expert motioned for Darcy to sit on the bed.

Jon sat beside her and patted her back. "We'll help any way we can."

Cole stood in front of them with Leslie at his elbow. He waited for Darcy to blow her nose. "First, I need to know who suggested you use CJI Investigations."

Jon relaxed. "Is that all? That's easy. It was that actor guy, Gerald Payne. 'Course, I didn't know you were CJI Investigations. And Darcy only met Ms. Leslie."

Jon shook his head like someone trying to clear away the remnants of a nightmare. "I went back down there the night Karren disappeared. I thought maybe I misunderstood what time I was supposed to pick her up. Payne said if she was missing—and he thought she must be, she was supposed to stay and clean up—that I should contact CJI. He said they—I guess he meant you—had a reputation for finding runaways, and maybe you could find Janice. I mean Karren." He ducked his head and wiped at his cheek with the back of his hand. "She liked Karren best, but I never called her that. I wish I had."

Darcy sniffed and squeezed back her tears. "I've been very confused about why Gerald Payne sent us to you. How did he know she would be in your room? Why did he send us to you if he didn't know she would be in your room?" She looked at the floor and shook her head. "So confusing."

Cole said, "I'm a little confused myself, but you've been a big help. Just one other question. Did either of you know she was working as a stand-in for Molly?"

Jon nodded. "I didn't know what it was called, but I knew when she had her hair bleached and got the blue contacts that she looked a lot like Ms. Heitkamp. At first I thought it was for a play about the Heitkamps or something. But you know something? When I found out the dead woman looked a lot like Ms. Heitkamp, I never thought it might be Karren."

Darcy dabbed at her eyes again. "She wrote that she had a part-time acting job. That's all she told me."

Cole said, "I'm sorry we had to bother you. Are you going back to San Antonio right now?"

Darcy stood up and began dropping miniature shampoo, soap, and mouthwash into her makeup bag. "No, we were raised in a little town outside San Antonio. There's a family plot at Helotes. We're having her . . . the body shipped to San Antonio. I suppose the funeral home will take it from there."

Cole motioned to Leslie. "You've been a big help. We'll let you know what we find out."

Jon's voice started out smooth, but shook with outrage by the time he finished talking. "If I catch that sorry bastard first, he's not going to live to get to a trial."

When Cole and Leslie got back in Leslie's car, she said, "I don't understand anything about what we just did."

Cole looked at his watch. "I'm not sure, but I think I'm onto something. Just hang in there with me. If I'm wrong, we may end up looking like a big bag of bologna."

"And if you're right?"

"If I'm right, we catch a murderer, save a political race, make headlines, and get to keep our job."

The blue-and-white awning valiantly held the sun off the top corner of the door, but the poster on the door had slowly surrendered its color to the attack of ultraviolet rays. For a late afternoon, it was hotter than any summer Cole remembered. They parked near the entrance to the theater and didn't waste any time getting inside to the cool air. Ruth Golden was halfway down the stairs by the time they crossed the lobby.

She beamed at Cole. "I hate those machines. I would have told you sooner, but I won't talk on the blasted contraptions."

Cole had no idea what she was talking about and wasn't sure he ever would. "Excuse me?"

She met them at the bottom of the stairs and shooed them toward the faded chairs in the lobby. "Your secretary—Harriet?"

"Henrietta," Leslie interjected.

Ruth shot her a "shut-up" glare, then smiled at Cole. "She said she'd tell you I remembered something that could be important, and that you'd get here as soon as you could."

Cole smiled back. "We aim to please." If Ruth remembered anything, he was sure she'd immediately forget it or scramble it.

Ruth moved a stack of programs to the middle of the desk and perched on the edge. She leaned forward and whispered. "It's about the night of the murder."

When Leslie pulled a notepad from her handbag, Ruth scowled. Cole extracted his pad and pen from his pocket and leaned toward Ruth. She looked at each of them. "Ready?"

They nodded in unison.

Ruth took a deep breath and expelled a single word. "Teal."

Leslie's puzzled expression matched Cole's feeling. He said, "Ma'am?"

Ruth bobbed her gray head. "Teal. I know teal when I see it. That strange woman was wearing a teal silk blouse and white dirndl skirt."

Cole tried to piece together her conversation with Henrietta. Evidently, she had told Henrietta she had seen someone in the theater on the night of the murder, and Henrietta must have directed her to be prepared to describe the woman to Cole when he arrived. He hated to break Ruth's confidence in the efficiency of his office. "Could you tell it to me from the top?"

Ruth clapped her hands together and grinned. "I knew she wasn't listening real close. Got it confused, didn't she? She'd never make it on the stage."

Leslie cleared her throat. "Ms. Golden, tell us about the woman in the teal blouse."

Ruth scowled at Leslie and looked back at Cole. "Is it okay if she hears this?"

Cole nodded. As far as he was concerned, it was okay for anyone to hear it except the woman in the teal blouse.

Ruth rose to the clandestine occasion. "It was after the show, see? Everything—well, almost everything—was put away, and just about everyone had left. There was a light on in the hall—I think Jerry was still in Room Three—and a couple of the other rooms were occupied."

Cole scribbled a doodle or two on his pad and looked up. "Was she from the audience?"

Ruth shook her head so violently she almost fell off the desk. "I look at every member of the audience and the cast. With my trained eye for clothing, I would have spotted a repeat in a gnat's breath."

Cole leaned back in the tweed chair and crossed his ankles out in front of him. "Did she do anything in particular that made you suspicious?"

"I passed the hallway to come out here and saw her opening the door to Room Five. The only reason I thought about it today was the new teal material Mrs. Windslow got for our pillows in the upstairs parlor. She shouldn't have been there."

Cole rubbed his head. "Mrs. Windslow shouldn't have been where?"

Ruth cackled and rocked back on the desk. "You are a mite slow, Mr. March. No, not Mrs. Windslow. The woman in the teal silk. She shouldn't have been in the hall. And especially, she shouldn't have been going in Room Five."

Leslie was writing rapidly. "Exactly why is that, Ms. Golden?"

"Because that room's reserved. Only certain outside actors and actresses can use it. That's where that tart got all gussied up for the photographers to take Molly Heitkamp's picture at our dress rehearsal." She grinned sheepishly. "I guess I shouldn't have told you about her doing spots for Molly." She dropped her voice to a whisper. "It's supposed to be a big secret."

She sat up straighter; a look of concentration rippled across her wrinkles. She cocked her head to one side. "Now that she's dead, I guess it doesn't make any difference."

Cole stifled an impulse to rush her. "I had already uncovered that piece of information, Ms. Golden, so you didn't spill the beans. Do you remember anything else about her?"

Ruth nodded. "I've seen her somewhere else. Not here. She's been in the papers. Society, maybe. Maybe with the governor. Not an actress, though. I'm sure of that. I know all of them."

Leslie looked up from her notes. "Could she have been a friend of Molly's?"

Ruth jiggled her feet. "Don't know. Don't think so, but don't know why not."

Cole got to his feet. "We'd like to see Room Five." He started toward the hallway. "And maybe some of the others for comparison."

A young man and two ladies came in the front door. They

greeted Ruth and rushed upstairs. The phone rang. Ruth picked it up and listened. "Eight," she said, and hung up. "You'd think they'd check the curtain times listed in the paper."

As they filed down the hall, Gerald came toward them. "Well, well, Mr. January," he said. "Back to snooping, I see."

Ruth grabbed Gerald's sleeve when he tried to pass them. "You're just the one I wanted to see." She pulled a ring of keys from her skirt pocket. "Show them Room Five."

Payne shrugged. "They're all alike, but whatever you say, Ruthie."

They were all alike in size, Cole noted, but from there each room took on a distinct personality. Stark and utilitarian, Room Five was the antithesis of Gerald's room, with its delicate decor and pastel colors. A few decorator props, looking out of place and abandoned, were stacked in the corner near the bare dressing table. Two lightbulbs were out on the left-hand row around the mirror. Beside the doorway, where the door swung against it, was a column about three feet high that could have held anything from a fern to a statue. A clean oval spot on the top was surrounded by dusty corners.

Payne brushed away the dust. "Wonder where Ruthie put the bust. We're going to need it in our fall production."

Cole inspected the dresser, pulling out empty drawers and running his hand back under them. He glanced up at Payne. "What bust?"

"The bust of Shakespeare that's usually on this stand."

Leslie peeked out from behind the dressing screen. "When was the last time you saw it?"

Payne shook his head. "I haven't had any reason to be in here in several weeks. Maybe a month or more." He started backing out the door. "If you want to see anything else, let me know. I'll be in my room. Room Three."

When Cole heard Payne's door close, he said, "Leslie, you go check with Ruth Golden. See what you can find out about the bust. I'm going to make a quick phone call."

▽

16

"IS THAT ALL she said?" Cole asked when Leslie came back down to the lobby.

Leslie cocked her hand on her hip and tilted her head to one side. "No, Cole, that's not all she said. I'm withholding information just to get your goat." She threw up both hands and sighed. "Yes, that's all she could remember. It was there a couple of weeks ago. She didn't know it wasn't there now. She suggested we ask Mrs. Windslow when she gets here."

Cole had hoped Leslie could help Ruth remember what happened to the statue. If no one missed it until now, it could have been the murder weapon. Or it could have been stored or stolen weeks before the murder. He held the front door open for Leslie. "What do you think?"

Leslie stormed out the door. "I think the old lady's batty. If the bust was stolen or if it was used to kill Karren, somebody should have realized it was missing."

While she backed the car from the curb, Cole noticed she was gritting her jaw hard enough to crush a walnut. He opened his mouth to say something, anything, to calm her.

She stabbed the brake and stared at him. "Don't say a word, Coleman January. Not a single word. Nothing. Just listen. We're going to call Lieutenant Harris and tell him that we suspect a bust of Shakespeare was the blunt object that Karren got slugged with." She backed into the street and drove toward the freeway.

Cole nodded. "Good idea. Sorry I didn't think of it myself. We'll make the call from A. J. Wilson's Chevrolet."

Leslie changed lanes ahead of a horn-blower and made it through the light before it turned red. "How can you think about buying a car at a time like this? We've practically got the killer in our hands and you want to go to"—she mocked the song used in the dealer's commercial—"A. J. Wilson's Chevrolet Sale-ah-ah-ah-arama."

Before he told the salesman he had arrived, Cole used the courtesy phone and called Lieutenant Harris. Leslie stood near his shoulder and leaned toward the receiver. He could feel her breath catching the outer rim of his right ear. A shiver passed through him. For a split second he wondered who he was calling and why.

When Harris came on the line Cole said, "There used to be a bust of Shakespeare on a pedestal in the room the victim used at the theater."

Harris chuckled. "Really on top of things, aren't you, January? We've had that statue in custody a while now."

Cole cursed under his breath. "So much for working together. You gonna tell me what you found?"

"We checked it over. Clean. No prints; no blood; no hair. The old boy should have quite a story to tell, though. I think it's been around for a long time and seen the secret lives behind the scenes."

Cole said, "I plan to be around for a long time, too. You got any more tidbits to pass out or do I have to beg for them too?"

"Just that somebody out there doesn't like you, January."

Cole drummed his fingers on the shelf below the phone. "Coming from you, that doesn't surprise me. If I find what I think I will in the next twenty-four hours, I'll let Fraizer and Johnson make the collar."

He hung up on Harris's huffing and sputtering, and turned to Leslie. She was gone. Cole's gaze darted across the showroom, then probed the glass-walled cubicles of the salesmen's offices. She was in the one near the front, talking and laughing with the man who sat behind the small desk. Cole didn't like the way the man was looking at her.

When Cole entered the tiny office, Leslie smiled up at him. "I told him you were here to pick up the red Silverado. Right?"

The man lifted a stack of papers from the middle of his desk and shook them at Cole. "Got a little paperwork first, partner, then that baby's all yours. I already sent it through make-ready."

The new-car smell brought a smile to Cole's lips. He probably shouldn't have gone all out, but the insurance payoff on the old Luv had given him his best shot at a jazzy buggy. It was late enough in the day that he didn't need the air conditioner, but muggy enough that he ran it anyway—with the moon roof open. He liked riding high above the sports cars he passed. He felt on top of everything, ready to strum heads if he had to. Whatever it took, somebody was going to talk. And that somebody just might be a blue-eyed blond.

Now that Molly didn't have a bodyguard, Cole could say he had to keep a closer eye on her. If she was still at the country club, she better have his guest pass ready.

The tall columns on each side of the gate supported the wrought-iron arch above. The large letters spelled out "Memorial West Country Club"; below that, small block letters warned, "Members Only." Cole grinned as he drove under the sign.

When he told the guard at the gatehouse who he was joining, he got a terse smile and wave-through to the white brick clubhouse. He parked the Silverado on the last row in the parking lot, close to the exit.

In the foyer, he signed the guest register and was directed to the dining hall. He sauntered under the crystal chandelier, past the original oil paintings, through the third arch. The pink-and-aqua room contained a few large round tables and several smaller ones. Most were occupied, but Cole didn't see Molly. He worked his way toward a small vacant table by the window. As he pulled out the chair, a waiter tapped his shoulder and pointed.

Cole ambled toward the table in the corner where Molly and Ruben sat with another couple. He dropped his hand on Molly's shoulder and smiled. "Hope I'm not interrupting anything."

"Hello, Mr. Cole January. So, you decided to join us after all." Molly pointed to the woman across from her. "This is the man I was telling you about."

After introductions all around and an invitation to join the group, Cole pulled a chair from another table and sat between the two women. Alissa's hair was as dark as Ruben's, her eyes as blue as the sky. She was exotically beautiful, and closer to his age than Molly's.

She ran her gaze over Cole slowly while she toyed with the thick gold chain around her neck. Suddenly, she dropped the chain and leaned toward Molly. "He certainly is."

Cole's smile felt awkward, but he made sure his voice didn't show it. "If you're talking about my good looks, charm, and outstanding talents, I agree."

She laughed from deep in her throat. Her eyes danced; her full red lips outlined orthodontic-perfect, whiter-than-white teeth. In a sultry voice she crooned, "I'm sorry if I put you at a disadvantage. Molly told me you were a good man for the job. I believe you are. Anyone who would waltz in here like you just did has the balls of a Brahman bull."

Cole grinned at her; his adorable lopsided grin, he hoped. "I give it my all, Alissa. Work or play, I give it my all."

Even Ruben, serious as usual, smiled slightly. "I'm sure you do, Cole. To what do we owe the honor of your presence? Answers or questions?"

Cole leaned away from the table as the waiter set a glass of water in front of him. "A little of both. Is there somewhere Molly and I could confer in private?"

Ruben said, "That won't be necessary. Alissa and Charles are on our side and know the whole story. They can be trusted."

Cole looked at Molly.

She shrugged. "Whatever." Cole took a sip of the ice water

from the turquoise blown-glass goblet in front of him. "Have you received any more unusual mail?"

Molly shook her head. "And no other threats."

Cole looked into her clear blue eyes. "I have to know when you plan to release the information you have on your father."

Alissa's eyes sparkled with glee. "You mean Jackie-poo is up to his ass in alligators, and everyone's going to know?" She clapped her hands together. "I love it!"

Cole jerked back and shot a stare at Ruben. "I thought you said they knew the whole story."

Molly shook her head. "Most of it. How do I know you won't tell the press before we have everything in place?"

Cole's gaze was steady. "You don't."

Molly squirmed in her chair and pulled herself erect. "Okay. I can live with that. Here's how it goes. We have proof that he has most, if not all, nonbid jobs let by the city. We also suspect he has skimped on materials and paid off one of the inspectors on the new annex. We can't prove that."

Cole began the next question with trepidation. "And you think Judith Barnes has something to do with it?"

Charles spoke up, but very softly, almost a whisper. "I know she does."

Alissa ran her finger down the side of her glass, leaving a clear trail in the frosted condensation. "Whatever Judith wants, Judith gets. And she wants Jackie-poo and all the money, too."

Cole glanced at Alissa before turning back to Molly. "When will you expose him?"

"Thursday night. We've called a press conference for eight. That will give them plenty of time to edit it down for the ten o'clock news."

Cole stood up and leaned down to speak. "You've been a big help, really. But I've got a few other little items to check out." He shook hands, saving Molly's for last. He held her hand in his. He was growing less and less fond of her, but he still had a job to do. "I suggest you stay with Ruben for the next couple of days. Your place may not be safe."

Molly looked up at him and smiled indulgently. "Thank you, Cole, but I've already made arrangements to stay with Alissa and Charles."

Cole winked at Ruben. "Don't say I didn't try."

Ruben gave him a quick nod. "Your efforts are noted and appreciated."

Cole drove straight to the office. It was one of the few times he wished he had a car phone. Nothing was urgent enough for him to stop and use a pay phone, but he was anxious to hear what Leslie had uncovered. Maybe he'd break down and get one of those portable cellulars after this case was wrapped up.

As he pulled into his parking slot at the rear of the building, he was surprised to see Henrietta's van and Leslie's car still in the lot. Not that they didn't ever work late. They did. Often. But he'd planned on having the office all to himself until he had a chance to talk to Fraizer.

Cole opened the office door to an eerie silence. No one was in the reception area. He heard paper rattling. Fraizer grunted. Leslie sneezed. He stuck his head into Leslie's office and grinned. "What's up?"

Leslie and Fraizer jerked their heads around. Fraizer said, "You could've knocked."

Cole entered the room. "In case you've forgotten, this is my office."

Leslie straightened the papers in front of her. "We're all a little jumpy, Cole. Take it easy." She dabbed at her nose with a tissue. "Actually, you claim this room is my office."

Cole leaned down on the conference table Leslie used for a desk. "And what, pray tell, has you two a little jumpy? And why are you sneezing?" He stepped back from the table. "And where's Henrietta?"

"Watch out. I'm right behind you, Coleman." She wheeled into Leslie's office with a roll of facsimile paper in her lap.

Cole threw up his hands. "Okay, gang, I give up. Somebody want to tell me what's going on?"

Henrietta grinned. "Probably nothing. I had this idea, see? My buddy at the *Chronicle* is going to fax me some old articles, and I've got to put a fresh roll of paper in the machine."

"Fine, just fine! I'm trying to solve a murder 'cause I don't want any more bodies in my bedroom, and you're reading old newspapers." He stomped through the outer office to his cubicle, then stomped back. He pointed at Leslie and glared. "Don't you dare get sick. I've got plans for us this weekend. And another thing!" He pointed at Fraizer. "I've got a new Silverado I want to show off."

Fraizer rocked back in his chair. "Now that's important!"

Cole waited for Fraizer to get to his feet. When he didn't, Cole folded his arms and glared at him. "The ladies have already seen it."

Fraizer scooted his chair back from Leslie's desk. "Then I guess it's up to me, ladies. If I don't go look, he'll pout for days."

Henrietta said, "How could we tell?"

Fraizer followed Cole to the parking lot, whining that everyone in the world had a new vehicle but him and the department said he had to wait another year. As they neared the Silverado, Fraizer said, "Have you talked to Leslie about Hoss's benefactor?"

Cole brushed a pine needle off the shiny hood. "Not yet. Why?"

Fraizer circled the truck and nodded approvingly. "She'll tell you."

"Where's Rose?"

"On her way. She had to take her mom to her sister's."

Cole opened the door. "Take a whiff of that."

Fraizer leaned into the truck. "Definitely new-car smell. Could have been someone from the mayor's office."

"What? Oh, you mean the mayor could have paid Hoss's bail?"

"Something like that. No proof, but we've got a tracer on it. Should know something in the next half hour."

When they returned to the office, Henrietta was watching for the incoming fax.

Leslie snorted into a tissue. "I think it's just allergies. I'll stop by the drugstore on the way home. I promise I won't be sick when Kevin gets here."

Fraizer rocked back on his heels, his arms folded across his chest. "Funny thing, allergies. Now, take my mother-in-law, for—"

Cole shot a quick glance at Henrietta. She shook her head, but he couldn't resist. "—for a day, a week, a year. Anybody, just take her."

Henrietta tooted the horn on her chair arm. "Two points!" She shrugged at Fraizer's scowl. "Sorry. What were you saying about your wife's poor mother and her allergies?"

Fraizer grunted. "Just that she takes the damn shots every week and they seem to help."

Leslie nodded. "Thanks, Fraizer, I'll look into it. Don't you think your fellows should have some answers for us by now?"

▽

17

FRAIZER PICKED UP the phone and punched in the numbers. After only a few words and several minutes of listening, he hung up. He flipped his big hands open palms-up. "He said the money for Hoss's bond was sent over from A-Wink Bail Bonds. Their dispatcher claims a delivery service brought in an envelope with the cash. A-Wink has a tracer on it and should be able to tell us who picked it up and where."

Cole wasn't surprised. He suspected the cash came from Hacksaw or the Strangler. Even if Hoss was the mayor's pet, it was unlikely she'd go his bail. That would look too bad on her record. He looked up at Fraizer. "Anything else?"

Fraizer shook his head. "No, they'll call if they find the slip, but I don't think we can count on it."

The facsimile machine rang, beeped, and started rolling. As the cover sheet came out, Henrietta glanced at it and dropped it in the trash. The next sheet she studied briefly and passed to Cole.

Cole held the slick paper under the light. The headline read, "Insurance Fraud Foiled." Cole tugged his eyebrows together. "Henrietta, why is he sending you these clips on the old Ross case? Don't I have copies in the file?"

She tilted her head to one side and grinned up at him. "I thought we might find some other pithy prose to pass on to the papers that wasn't in your file."

"Don't tell me the reporters are still hounding you."

Leslie stretched her arms across the table and lowered her head against it. "Do you need me tonight?"

Cole couldn't prevent the worry from crossing his face, but he quickly erased it from his voice. "More than you'll ever know, but you go home and get some rest." Her eyes were watery, but he saw the acknowledging smile.

Henrietta counted off on her fingers. "Drink plenty of fluids. Take two aspirin. Call him in the morning. That ought to make everyone healthy."

Fraizer looked from one to the other. "I don't get it. Why are you all laughing?"

Cole captured Leslie's hand as she went past him. "Don't worry, Big Boy, someday you'll be old enough to understand."

As Cole and Leslie walked behind the building toward her car, Cole said, "Do you want me to stop by on my way home? I could bring you some chicken soup, or whatever."

She grimaced. "Yuck! No, thanks. I'm not helpless. I just need to rest and take that antihistamine that almost knocks me out. I'll be fine. Promise." She gave Cole a quick kiss on his cheek.

When Cole walked back into the office, Fraizer was grinning like a ten-year-old looking at his first *Playboy*. "Cole, you mother frog, you. I thought you were the one that said business and pleasure don't mix."

Cole didn't know what Henrietta had told Fraizer, but he could guess. He didn't mind. "They don't. When we work, we work; when we play, we play. We don't mix 'em."

Fraizer nodded and rocked back on his heels. "The day you told me you hired her, I said you'd end up falling for her. And you said she was just a kid. Ha!"

Henrietta said, "Kid or no kid, she's a good investigator. She doesn't put up with any crap out of Cole or anybody else."

Fraizer said, "Like Rose and my wife don't put up with my nonsense, huh?"

Cole said, "Speaking of the lovely flower, what's taking her so long? I thought you said she was on her way here."

Henrietta stacked the facsimile pages and stapled them together. "While you were outside with Leslie, she called. She's about five minutes from here."

Cole said, "In that case, I'll wait till she gets here to tell you what I found out from Molly."

Fraizer leaned back against the wall. "Does Harris know?"

Cole shook his head. "After what he pulled, he can wait for this one."

Rose pounded on the front door as she opened it. "Police! Open up!"

Henrietta rolled into the outer office to meet her. "Damn you, Rose, you promised not to do that anymore. The neighbors already think we're weird."

Rose snapped her fingers. "Damn, I can't imagine where they got that idea. Where's Roy?"

Cole and Fraizer sauntered out of Leslie's office like truant school boys. Cole said, "We're working out the details of the collar I'm going to let you two claim."

Rose's eyes got wide. "Oh, really? What makes you think we need your help?"

"Have you brought anybody in?"

She leveled a finger at him. "Good point. What do you have?"

Cole ticked off his data. "Whoever moved the body has to be strong. Whoever killed Karren probably thought she was Molly. Strong men so far? Hoss, the Strangler, and Jon O'Connell. Hoss doesn't have a motive I can identify, except maybe to protect the Strangler. The Strangler is strong enough to carry a body and doesn't need any help from Hoss. Jon's sister was the victim. I'm convinced he didn't do it."

Rose elbowed Cole aside for the spotlight. "And I say whoever killed Karren didn't mean to kill anybody."

Cole countered, "Aha, but can you prove it? Someone fully intended to deter someone from something."

Fraizer said, "It didn't take much strength to swing that statue, if it was the weapon. Once it got moving, it could pack a deadly blow. How do you know—"

Henrietta squeezed the bulb on her horn. "Time out! Cole, you have something to tell us."

Cole ducked his head and thought a minute. "Oh, yeah.

Molly. She's exposing all the evil doings of her father, or rather her stepfather, at a press conference Thursday night."

Rose's mouth fell open. "I knew she was supporting Gomez, but I didn't think she'd stoop to mudslinging at a member of her own family."

Fraizer said, "Stepfather? That's the first I heard she wasn't Jack Heitkamp's own daughter. Puts a whole new light on the subject. I should've hauled him in the night I saved your sorry ass from that trespassing charge."

Henrietta pointed at Fraizer. "I gotta hand it to you, Fraizer, you have a way with words. And you think the new light on the subject says the man could've clubbed her with the statue, thinking it was Molly? Don't you think anyone who lived with Molly since she was two years old would know a stand-in from the real thing?"

Cole winked at her. "What say we go arrest Mr. Jack Heitkamp."

Fraizer's expression was pained. "Now hold on, Mother Frog. I don't know that we have any grounds to pick him up, just yet. What's Molly claiming he did?"

"Just getting all the nonbid and most of the bid jobs from the city and possibly scattering a little payola to some city inspectors. Cuts costs if you don't have to bring every little thing up to spec." Cole grabbed the facsimile cover sheet out of the trash and stuffed it in his pocket. "While you think it over, I've got to go see a man about a mule. I suggest all of you go home and get some sleep."

Cole could see they weren't getting anywhere tossing ideas between themselves. What he needed was a new slant. Something to drive the killer out of hiding. Something to make him sweat. Until he could figure what little thing was tripping him up, he'd have to stir somebody's stew and hope to find some meat in it.

On Westheimer, Cole pulled into the parking lot of an all-night print shop that boldly posted their cheap fax rate. He filled out most of the required cover sheet, then stopped when he came to the destination line. He drew the crumpled sheet from his pocket. Sending a message to the *Chronicle* should start something rolling besides fax paper.

He wrote, "Molly Jones-Heitkamp look-alike murder solved. Suspect soon in custody."

With that taken care of, he took the 610 Loop south until he connected with the Southwest Freeway. Although the construction crews kept traffic bottlenecking down to one or two lanes, it was still the quickest way to Kirby Drive and the ACT. This was not a time for his zigzag route.

By the time he dropped off the freeway, he had replayed the facts in his head. The one question that haunted him was still there: Why was the body deposited in his room? Since he knew Jon got his name from Gerald Payne, he had to know where Payne got it. Payne had to have told Jon before Cole ever went to the theater. Cole had no delusions about his own reputation. It was good, but not that good. Anyone outside the insurance industry had a better-than-average chance of never having heard his name. Except for the Ross case eight years ago, he'd never made headlines in either paper.

The curtain was going up on the third act when Cole arrived. The house was slightly more than half full. He eased through the casually dressed group of theatergoers to the hallway behind the staircase. One of the ushers tried to stop him, but he convinced the young woman that Gerald Payne was expecting him and would be very disappointed if he didn't show up. Might even ruin Gerald's performance if she didn't let him in.

Cole threw open Payne's dressing room door. Payne, in costume, was on the phone. He slapped his hand over the mouthpiece and glared at Cole. "What the hell are you doing here? Get out!"

Cole stepped into the small room and quietly closed the door behind him. His voice was level and calm. "You're going to tell me what I want to know, or you won't finish the show tonight."

Payne spoke quickly into the phone. "We'll talk later. I have to go."

As he lowered the dainty antique French receiver, he squinted his eyes and clenched his jaw. "I have less than ten minutes before I go on. Please be quick."

The request was not polite. In fact, it was not a request. Cole didn't take demands very well on a good day, and this was not a good day. "I'll take however long it takes. Now, what say you tell me how come you gave my name to Jon when his sister was missing?"

"It's quite simple, really. I had heard you were very good at finding missing persons." He dropped to the satin-covered dresser stool and picked up a small white powder puff. "Now, if you'll excuse me, I have to prepare for the last scene."

In two steps Cole crossed the room. He grabbed Payne's shoulders and lifted him to his feet. Payne was heavier than he looked. "No, Mr. Payne, I won't excuse you. Where did you hear that I'm good at finding missing persons?"

Payne blanched paler than the powder puff. "Get your hands off me, Mr. January, or I shall be forced to call for assistance."

Cole released him and shoved him back on the stool. "Why don't you just do that? But before you do, you might want to think about what I'll tell anyone who comes to your aid."

Cole could see the actor donning another character. An agile, aloof personality. Detached. Disinterested.

Payne drew himself erect. "I hardly think anyone in this theater would believe anything derogatory about me that you could fabricate. I have no time for this nonsense."

Cole couldn't prevent his hands from forming fists. He shook one under Payne's chin. "You're gonna talk. Now!"

Payne clamped his lips together and patted his nose with the puff.

Cole swung. Not especially hard, but hard enough to unseat Payne.

Payne scrambled to his feet, a terrified wild-animal look in his eyes. It took him more than a second to regain his composure. "See here, Cole January, I will not be intimidated or bullied. I have nothing to say to you."

There was a sharp tap at the door, followed by a crisp "Five minutes."

Cole grabbed Payne's arm as he started for the door. "You're not leaving this room until you answer me."

Panic in Payne's eyes, his rapid breathing, his squirming against Cole's grip—nothing produced any sympathy from Cole. The seconds slipped by. Payne took a deep breath and sighed it out. "Very well. I read about you in the newspaper."

Cole squeezed his arm. "That's a lie, Payne. Where?"

"You're hurting my arm."

"I know. Where?"

"A friend. A friend said you might help Jon find his sister."

"A name, Payne. A good name." He squeezed harder.

"Andrews. Nathan Andrews."

The shock of the answer rippled through Cole. Of all the people he had met on this case, he would never have put those two men in the same room. "Where can I find Mr. Andrews?

Payne jerked his arm free. "Honestly, Mr. January. How should I know? I occasionally run into him at the Purple Panther Lounge."

The tap on the door was stronger this time. "Two minutes."

Cole flashed a plastic grin. "Break a leg."

Cole had heard of the Purple Panther, a bar on Westheimer inside the Loop dedicated to protecting the rights of gays. He had no quarrel with that, but he also had no desire to go there. He doubted if Nathan Andrews aka Hoss would be there tonight. Whoever bailed him out of jail would keep him on a short leash.

As late as it was, Cole knew it would be pointless to keep pushing. An early start Wednesday morning could be just as fruitless. In spite of the erratic demands of his career, he insisted on keeping to his routine whenever possible. Nightly sleep was rule one; rule two was making his morning run.

By midmorning he was physically alert and mentally organized. Fraizer had said the mayor's office might have something to do with the bail, but Cole headed for Mid-Town Gym and Training Club. Hacksaw kept up with the players. If he didn't pay the bond for Hoss, he would know who did.

When Cole turned the corner at the convenience store next to Mid-Town Gym, he saw three police cars, roof lights flashing, parked at odd angles. One officer waved him around the area while another held off oncoming traffic. As he eased past the scene, thinking another drive-in grocery had been robbed, he saw the yellow crime-scene tape. Another convenience-store manager had shot back.

About a half a block past the scene, Cole parked in front of a vacant store space and walked back to the gym. Hacksaw was talking with a detective, who nodded to Hacksaw's answers. Cole approached them, his insides churning with apprehension.

Hacksaw's cheeks were shiny with tears. The pain in his heart was etched in his furrowed brow. He wiped at a fresh tear running toward his chin and choked out the words, "Drive-by. He never had a chance."

▽

18

COLE DIDN'T HAVE to ask who. The pain on Hacksaw's face said everything he didn't want to hear. He put his hand on Hacksaw's arm. "I'm sorry, Hacksaw. I know how you felt about him."

The detective glanced up at Cole, then made a mark on the small notepad he held. One wisp of his yellow hair fluttered across his forehead, and he brushed it aside with the end of his pen. He didn't look up when he spoke. "Were you a friend of this Nathan Andrews?"

Cole shook his head. "No, I met him once or twice. Were there any witnesses?"

Hacksaw said, "No, man, I didn't even know he was coming in today."

The detective looked at him and scratched his temple with the end of the pen. "Why is that?"

Hacksaw folded his massive arms across his bare chest. "He hadn't been in for a few days. I figured he was out of town."

It was evident to Cole that Hacksaw wasn't going to tell the man anything about Hoss being in jail. The good, respectable life hadn't erased his old don't-help-the-law philosophy.

The detective made a note. "Did he go out of town often?"

Hacksaw rubbed the sweat off his face and refolded his arms. "No . . . I don't know. All I know is he came here every day to work out, except for the days he went to the Youth Help Alliance to work with the kids. He'd changed. I could count on him."

While the detective made notes between scratching his temple and asking questions, Cole wondered if maybe Fraizer was right and he was wrong. If he was wrong about that, he was wrong about Hacksaw all the way around. Hacksaw would have been expecting Hoss if he'd had anything to do with getting him out of jail. Or maybe Hacksaw *had* bailed Hoss out and the tears were all a big lie. No, Cole couldn't swallow that. It had to be someone else. Maybe bail did come from the mayor or someone connected with her office. Or maybe it came from someone who wanted Hoss out where they could find him.

Cole's mind plunged ahead like a bobsled in an ice chute. Thoughts banged into each other, creating more questions. When Hoss agreed to teach street kids to wrestle through the Youth Help Alliance, it was a trade-off. What was the trade? Back to jail or rehab? For what? Was there any connection, other than the Strangler's friendship, to Karren's murder?

Cole didn't realize he was staring into space as if he were searching for answers on the gym window. He jumped when the detective touched his shoulder.

The detective pointed his pen at Cole. "I said, when did you last meet Mr. Andrews?"

Cole pulled his business card from his pocket. "Cole January," he said. He decided it wouldn't be prudent to tell the detective he'd questioned Hoss at the city jail. "I met him here earlier this week when I was working on a case." He thought it was ironic how the meaning of the phrase "working on a case" had changed. It used to mean trying to expose someone in an insurance scam. He couldn't figure out why he was thrust into this nasty business of murder.

The detective tapped Cole's card with his pen. "What kind of case, January? Might have started something. Know what I mean?"

Cole expressed what he hoped was an understanding smile and nod. "It didn't have anything to do with Mr. Andrews. I was looking for a friend of his. Turned out he was in the hospital. The friend. Not Mr. Andrews."

Hacksaw cleared his throat. "Uh, if you don't need me, I'll just get back inside."

The detective nodded his okay, then shoved Cole's card between the back pages of his notebook. He winked at Cole. "Don't go leaving town on me. I get nervous when a PI knows a victim. Might have another question or two I haven't thought up yet. Know what I mean?"

Cole had no intention of leaving town. "If I can be of any help, just let me know. Know what I mean?"

Cole knew from the detective's congenial smile that the man had completely missed the mockery. He also knew it would be only a few hours at most before the detective and the rest of HPD discovered Cole had filed a complaint against Hoss, then talked to him before he was let out on bail.

The narrow street was filling up fast. Cole saw two TV news crews pushing through the crowd, shoving mikes in front of stunned faces. He didn't wait for them to single him out. At a near-jog, he parted the collected audience and made it to his Silverado in time to catch a teenager trying to pop a Slim-Jim down his window. The kid hightailed it between buildings, leaving Cole wondering if the CD-player option was such a good idea.

Right now the only good idea he had was to go someplace where he would be safe enough to think.

Cole drove straight to Benny's Burritos. The big bowl of steaming chili settled like a brushfire in the pit of his stomach. The phone was still out of order. When he complained to Benny, the restaurant owner led him to the back office and pointed to a black rotary-dial telephone. "You got three minutes. Well—for you, maybe five."

Cole thanked him. Was it good looks or his charm that had earned the favor? Only family or other Hispanics were normally allowed in back. He dialed slowly, wondering if he was doing the right thing. If he woke her, she'd be angry. If he didn't call, she might be angrier. Sick people needed rest; that was common sense. He pushed the hang-up button.

Maybe he shouldn't bother her. In the next instant, he ignored common sense and dialed again.

When Leslie answered, sleep clouded her voice. Cole was tempted to hang up, but he wanted her to know he was concerned. He also wanted to bring her up to date. Most of all, he needed to hear her voice.

"How are you feeling?"

She groaned. "Okay, I guess. I felt better before I had to answer the phone."

"I'm sorry. I thought you'd want to know that someone shot and killed Hoss."

"My God, Cole. Why?"

"I think he may have carried the body. If the Strangler was too drunk, or so drunk he didn't know what he'd done, Hoss may have cleaned up the mess to keep his friend out of trouble."

"And you think the Strangler killed him to keep him quiet?"

"Could be. I'm sorry I woke you, but—"

"No, that's okay. Anything I can do?"

"Yeah, call Misty Glen and see if Jimmy—they probably have him listed as James—Strauss went back there after we took him in for questioning."

"Where can I call you?"

"You can't. I'll check back with you later. Get some rest. Tomorrow may be a tough one."

As Cole hung up, a rolling burp erupted along with a string of ideas. Benny's chili was working again. He thanked Benny for the use of the phone and dropped an extra-large tip on the table as he left. He had one more phone call to make, but he didn't want to jinx it by using more than his allotted five minutes.

Cole spotted the pay phone on the outside west wall of a convenience store in the next block. He knew the plastic would be so hot it would feel soft. Using a few pages from the battered phone book chained to the shelf, he wrapped the receiver before he lifted it to his ear and dialed.

When Cole identified himself Henrietta said, "I'm sorry, Mr. January isn't here. I'd be glad to give him a message?"

Cole wasn't in the mood to play games or break codes. "I don't care who's there. Hoss has been killed and I need to know if Fraizer said where he was going."

"Excuse me? Did you say Menefee? Yessir, I've got it. Clark Menefee. 555-1300. I'll give him the message as soon as he arrives. Thank you."

"Henrietta! Stop! I've got to talk to you. Now!" The line went dead in his hand.

Cole stomped to the Silverado and jerked open the glove compartment. It didn't help his mood to find nothing there but the owner's manual. He slammed the truck door and barreled into the store. "Give me change for a dollar."

The man behind the counter said, "So sorry. No buy, no change."

Cole grabbed a package of gum from the impulse rack and slapped the dollar on the counter.

His mood hadn't improved when he returned to the phone. He dialed Leslie again and got the same sleepy croak. "Get your copy of Henrietta's code sheet!"

"Oh, Cole," she moaned, "I was having a great dream. Get what? Oh, sure. Hang on." The receiver clattered against a tabletop.

Cole jiggled the rest of the change in his pocket. He mopped the sweat from his head and neck. He squinted toward his truck and cursed himself for not getting everything out of the Luv. Just when he had given up and decided Leslie must have gone back to sleep, she said, "I've got it. What's the problem?"

"First tell me what you found out."

"The line was busy. I'll try again later."

"I know Menefee is men. Clark is reporters. What the hell does 1300 mean?"

"Uh . . . Here it is! I can't tell if it's call back or come back; or if it says three or there. There's some dried chocolate or something on it. How did you do a dumb thing like lose your code sheet?"

"It's got chili or something on it," he shouted. "How the hell do I know! Go back to sleep."

Leslie said, "This stuff will wear off in another hour. I promise, Cole."

Sweat soaked his shirt and rolled from his head toward his eyes. Cole dropped another quarter in the slot and dialed Henrietta again. Without giving her time to talk, he said, "I know the reporters are there. Just answer yes or no. Have they discovered I filed a complaint against Hoss?"

"Yes, that is correct. No, I don't know when he'll be here."

"Have you confirmed?"

"No sir, that won't be necessary."

"Are the cops looking for me?"

"Not as far as I know, but I'm sure it's a possibility."

"You don't do very well with a simple yes or no, do you?"

"I'll certainly try. Anything else I can tell him?"

"Yeah, tell him you need a raise, and he's a jerk if he doesn't give you one."

"Thank you, Mr. Menefee. I'll do that."

It was starting to come together. Another one of those elusive little things clicked into place. With his last piece of change he called one more number.

"Hacksaw, I know this is not a good time, but I gotta know something."

"You just did catch me, Bantam. I'm closing up."

"Was Hoss at the gym the first time I was there—when I was looking for that runaway kid?"

"You left before he came in. I know, 'cause he always comes in asking if anything happened he needs to know about. I told him some kid ran away and we had a PI named January check us out. I remember he said, 'I guess a dick named January is better than a pig named Friday.' " Hacksaw choked back the emotion that was creeping into his voice. "That's the only reason I remember. Does that help?"

"More than I can tell you. Thanks, Hacksaw."

Cole guessed if the cops wanted him, they would be looking for the old Luv. In the Silverado he would have a chance to finish what he started and maybe, just maybe, tie it all up in red, white, and blue.

Time moved faster than the Silverado. Cole had to make it to Leslie's before the cops discovered he had a new truck. He knew he couldn't risk going to his apartment or office. They might even be watching Leslie's, but it was a chance he would have to take. If he turned himself in, who would believe him? If Henrietta was able to get rid of the reporters and locate Fraizer and Johnson, they'd believe him.

When he dropped off the Southwest Freeway at Gessner, he had slim hope of contacting the detectives without alerting Homicide. He turned into the subdivision, praying it was too soon for anyone to think of watching Leslie's house. Time, as fast as it seemed to be traveling, was still on his side. So was luck.

Fraizer's car was parked in Leslie's driveway. Cole smiled. Now he owed them more than dinner. Maybe he'd throw in a magnum of champagne.

When he knocked on the door, Rose opened it and smiled at him.

Cole sighed. "You look better than Benny's best."

Leslie called out, "I heard that."

Cole walked toward the sound of her voice. "And I mean every word of it!"

Fraizer and Leslie were at the kitchen table, large glasses of iced tea in front of them. Rose scooted to the chair against the wall and motioned for Cole to join them.

Cole turned the chair around and straddled the seat. "Now isn't this a pretty sight. You three having a little tea social while Hoss Andrews gets gunned down in the street."

Fraizer said, "Yeah, we heard. Henrietta tracked us down just after it came in over the radio. We got over here as fast as we could—"

Rose finished his thought. "—and before they put out an

APB on you." She narrowed her eyes at Cole. "You know they'll put you on the suspect list, don't you?"

Leslie lifted her tea glass as she stood up. "I have a feeling I better get on my working duds."

Cole thought she looked just fine in the jeans and T-shirt. "You sure you feel like it?"

Leslie smiled and sniffed. "I've sheared sheep and branded cattle feeling worse."

After all the lectures she'd given him lately, he wasn't about to argue with her. And he was going to need all the help he could muster.

Fraizer rattled the ice in his drained glass. "January, you might want to know where Hoss's bail money came from, but it probably doesn't make any difference now."

Cole stared at Fraizer, waiting for the information. The big officer stared back. Rose slapped the table. "Fraizer! Tell him!"

Fraizer blinked. "Like I said, the mayor's campaign headquarters. Judith Barnes signed the dispatch slip."

Rose shrugged. "They couldn't let their project go down the tubes."

Cole rubbed his hands together. "Big Boy, you said the magic word. I may solve two murders."

The excitement of being close, so close, to wrapping it up had his heart racing. He checked his watch. Only a few hours till Molly's disclosure was scheduled to erupt on the evening news. If his luck held, he'd have everything in position before then.

A couple of phone calls later, Cole knew he'd been at his best. Convincing, that's what he was. He convinced Molly he had to see her before she went on the air. He convinced Fraizer to meet him where he thought the suspect would be at show time. He convinced Leslie that she was too sick to travel and that he needed her by the phone. After all that convincing, he still wasn't sure where he was headed until he took the exit ramp at Kirby.

He didn't know how soon he would make the suspect list,

but in the Silverado he felt safe. That was his first break. Pulling into the parking lot across from the All Citizens' Theater was the second. When he got out of the truck, there it was—a green Ford F-150 with the passenger side crumpled in. Red paint streaked the crinkled metal. He dashed across the street and threw open the theater door.

▽

19

MRS. WINDSLOW LOOKED up from behind the desk. "Why, Mr. January! What can I do for you?" She straightened the stack of programs in front of her.

Cole shifted his weight from one foot to the other. "There's a truck in the parking lot with its lights on. An F-150. Do you know who it belongs to?"

Mrs. Windslow smiled broadly. "Why, I believe that's Jerry's new truck."

Cole caught a flash of movement under the stairs. "Then he's here?"

"I haven't seen him, but I think I heard him go into his dressing room a short while ago. That's—"

Cole pointed toward the hallway. "Room Three?"

"Why, yes. You've certainly learned your way around here." She beamed at him. "Interested in working long hours for no pay as a stagehand?" Her deep laugh would have reached the back row from center stage.

Cole shook his head and walked toward the hallway. He crouched down and threw open the door to Room Three, half-expecting Payne to have a gun or spear aimed at his heart. The room was empty.

He raced back to the lobby. "Did he come through here?"

Mrs. Windslow was talking with one of the cast and nodded at Cole. "Be with you in just a minute, Mr. January."

Cole stepped in between them and shoved his face just inches from Mrs. Windslow's. "If Payne didn't come through here, where's the back door?"

She responded with a blank stare. "Good heavens, Mr. January, what's the matter with you?"

He felt as if he were talking to a statue. No matter what he said, she kept that blank, indifferent look. He pushed away from the desk. "I've got to—never mind." He was blasting out the door as he spoke.

The F-150 rumbled past Cole and veered toward a parked car before it straightened up. Cole raced to his truck, wishing he had on his Nikes. He jammed the key in the ignition and twisted it as he slammed the door. He could see Payne, if it was Payne, rounding the corner onto Kirby without slowing down for the stop sign. Horns blared; tires squealed.

Cole swung onto Kirby, grateful for the break in the traffic. The F-150 was in the lane entering the Southwest Freeway. Cole gunned the Silverado, cut in front of a sports car, and reached the lane only three cars behind the Ford. When the light changed, the F-150 turned right and shot into the feeder lane on the far left. Cole followed. Of the cars between them, only one remained. When the Ford entered the flow of the Southwest Freeway headed for downtown, the driver didn't look back. Cole stayed close, but didn't try to catch him or pull alongside. He hoped the driver would lead him to the murderer. So far, he thought they were going in the wrong direction.

That thought had no more than danced across Cole's mind when the Ford took the Greenbriar exit. The two trucks circled under the freeway and drove toward West Houston. On the turn, Cole positively identified the driver. His faith in his hunch was restored. If Payne knew he was still being followed, it didn't show. He tried no more reverses or devious detours.

Cole had been following him about twenty minutes, usually a couple of cars back, when Payne pulled off the freeway and into the parking lot of a strip center on Beechnut and the Southwest Freeway. Cole took the next entrance to the parking lot and slowly drove toward the green truck.

Payne stood beside it, shaking his fist at Cole. His face was contorted with fear and anger.

Cole rolled to a stop in front of him, then got out and sauntered toward him. "You got something you want to say to me, Payne?"

Payne sputtered. He stomped his foot. For a minute it looked as if he was going to swoon again. Then he did something Cole was completely unprepared for. He raised his hands over his head, turned, and faced his truck, then threw his hands down on the hood, spread his legs, and "assumed the position."

Cole said, "Don't be ridiculous. I'm not an officer. You're not armed. What say you tell me about the dents in this truck."

Payne lowered his head and mumbled, "I didn't want to do it. She made me."

"Who made you do what, Payne? Speak up. I can't hear you." He singsonged the last sentence, thinking that Henrietta would be pleased with the way he imitated Gomer Pyle's sergeant.

"She made me run you off the road. She thought you'd leave her alone. Let the cops handle it."

"How did she make you do it?"

"It was the only way." Payne paced in front of his truck, flailing his arms dramatically. "She said it was the only way she would get me the Esther Philmore grant money. It was that, or she would tell the police I killed that dumb bitch."

"Whoa! You want to tell me who, now, or do you want to wait till I beat it out of you?"

Payne whimpered. "Can we just go sit down somewhere and talk like gentlemen? I'm sweating."

They agreed to drive to the coffee shop at the corner. Cole hoped he wasn't being foolish. Once Payne was in the truck, he could decide to run again. Cole kept his fingers crossed and his eyes on Payne. They found parking places near each other and walked into the coffee shop together.

In a booth in the back, after the waitress brought two big iced teas, Payne started talking. "I heard a commotion in Room Five the night Karren was killed. When I burst in, the girl was on the floor. Blood everywhere. She threatened to go to the police and say I did it. Everyone knew Molly and I had argued. Over the grant." He lowered his eyes. "I guess I should have told you about that. Anyway, several people heard me curse her stand-in, too. I never liked Karren. She could be very difficult. Anyway, there was nothing I could do to bring her back. But it was when she threatened to call the police and pin the murder on me that I agreed to help her. We cleaned up all that blood, and I told her I wouldn't have anything more to do with it."

Cole thought of many things to say while Payne talked, but he was afraid if he interrupted him, he'd never get him going again.

Abruptly, Payne stopped talking, as if he expected Cole to speak. Cole still didn't know who *she* was, but was confident Payne would eventually tell him in his own way, when he got around to it. So instead of asking the same question again, Cole tried to pin down the information. "What did you actually hear before you went into Room Five?"

Payne dipped the lemon out of his tea and squeezed it again. "I thought she yelled, 'Look at me when I talk to you!' or something like that. Right after that, there was a thud. I guess it was Karren hitting the floor. Do you think I heard her head actually being hit?"

"Could be. Did you kill Hoss or did she?"

Payne rolled his eyes and turned pale. "Nathan? Nathan is dead? My God, when will it all end?" He pulled his knees up to his chest and hugged them. He rocked slowly, tears silently rolling down his face. His voice was a whispery monotone. "We were friends a long time ago. Good friends. We stayed in touch. He came to see me at the theater sometimes. We laughed about our young and foolish days." His eyes focused on the distant memory, as if he was trying to freeze each incident into a snapshot he could view again and again. Then it was over, the grieving done. Brief. Total.

He lowered his feet to the floor. "It was an accident. She didn't intend to kill the girl. Whoever killed Nathan, that was no accident."

"The jury will decide that. I think I know who we're talking about, but just so I don't go off half-cocked, what say you give me a name?"

▽

20

COLE BOUNCED OVER the potholes in the road, gripping the steering wheel of the Silverado to keep on course. At least he was on the right course, he thought. Now, at any rate. He never figured on Gerald Payne being so completely tangled in it all. The answers were unraveling like a moth-eaten sweater, and Cole didn't intend to get left out in the cold.

Henrietta promised she'd have someone meet him, even if she couldn't find Fraizer and Johnson. If nobody was home, ACT would be one actor short for the next performance.

When Cole pulled into the upper-middle-class neighborhood, he noticed a sedan tailing him. The glare from the low sun made it impossible to identify the driver. Whoever it was, he wasn't very good at discreet surveillance. Probably an amateur, Cole decided.

Now that he was prepared to confront the murderer, he wasn't worried about the tail. He consulted the hastily drawn map Payne had given him and read the green-and-white street sign. He'd been there before, but he'd entered the subdivision from a different street. One more block, turn right, according to the map.

The tail followed.

Cole slowed to a stop at the front walk. The tail parked behind him, blocking the driveway. Cole got out. The tail got out. The tail grinned.

Cole said, "Good to see you, Harris. And this time I mean it."

Lieutenant Harris nodded, jowls bobbing. "I wouldn't

miss this for anything short of Laticia's piano recital."

As they marched up the walkway, side by side, Harris said, "Sorry Fraizer and Johnson couldn't come. They're checking out a rumor that started at a print shop on Westheimer. Someone faxed a message to the morgue at the *Chronicle*. You wouldn't know anything about that, would you?"

Cole never missed a step. "Harris, I'm hurt that you would ask."

"Just wouldn't want you dropping a bomb like that in my lap."

"If you want to see a bomb, watch the Channel 11 news at ten. Molly's going to drop a real bomb that's going to have a lot of folks up all night."

"She's going to run instead of Gomez?"

"No, better." Movement inside the house caught his eye. He pointed to the window. "Check this out."

They could hear a TV or radio and see into the living room through the sheer curtains that covered the window. There she was in all her gilded glory. The unmistakable Judith R. Barnes weaved her way to the birdcage in front of the window. She held something in her right hand. A glass was Cole's first guess. The same small tumbler she was sipping from when he was there. She was talking to the white cockatoo, shaking her finger at it.

They watched a couple of minutes before Harris banged on the door. "Police! Open up!"

Judith pulled back the sheer curtains at eye level and held the lower part of the transparent material in front of her as if it could hide her. Cole watched recognition dawn slowly in her eyes. She smiled with half her mouth and wiggled a friendly finger at him.

When Judith opened the door she stumbled back, her hand still on the doorknob. She started to close it, but her grip slipped. She turned and zigzagged back to the right. She fell into the living room sofa. "Don't jus' stand there," she slurred, adjusting her shiny gold dress. It had shifted to unladylike heights. "Come join the party."

Cole looked at Lieutenant Harris and shrugged. Harris entered the foyer, his heels clicking on the marble.

Cole came in behind him, but circled around and stepped into the room first. "Where's the party? I hate to see a lady all dressed up with no place to go."

Judith sat a little straighter, listing to the east only slightly. "I perfectly well have a place to go. My gentleman friend has been detained."

Cole said, "I'll just bet he has. And he's probably going to be very late. I hear he's not moving from in front of his television set until after the news."

With as much indignation as she could muster, Judith squared her shoulder. "And just what does that mean?" Her hand waltzed the tumbler around in the air on its way to her lips.

Lieutenant Harris crossed the room and leaned down to her. "I'm Lieutenant Harris, Ms. Barnes—HPD. I wonder if we might ask you a few questions."

"You just ask your little old questions, Lieutenant, by all means. I have nothing to hide." She tugged the skirt down a fraction of an inch more.

Cole wondered if Harris was going to continue this polite line of interrogation or get on with it. So far, he calculated that two murders, and possibly a couple of other heinous crimes perpetrated against him, were directly connected to the pseudo–southern belle on the couch.

Harris's jaw was steady; his eyes were slits. "Where were you last Wednesday night, Ms. Barnes?"

She drained her glass before she answered. "Memory fails, Lieutenant. I'll have to consult my calendar." Judith slowly pulled herself up from the couch, then aimed for the wet bar. Beside the empty decanter was a fifth of Black Label.

Harris followed her. "Maybe this will improve your memory, Ms. Barnes."

There went the polite interrogation, Cole thought. Harris sounded just like he did when he chewed out Cole. "You were seen at the All Citizens' Theater after the dress rehearsal Wednesday night. Does that ring a bell, Ms. Barnes?"

Judith splashed Scotch into the tumbler and plopped in one ice cube from the stainless-steel ice bucket. She didn't bother to use the dainty tongs. "If I was seen there, I must have been there, don't you suppose, Lieutenant?"

Cole joined them at the bar and helped himself to a glass of water. He had never seen Harris in action against anyone but himself. This was fun.

Harris said, "What were you doing there *after* the show was over? Meeting a friend? Picking up gays? What?"

She turned on Harris like a mama lion protecting her cubs. She sounded almost sober. "See here, Lieutenant Harris, you can't just walk in here and talk to me like this. I demand to see my lawyer." She clamped her lips together in a nearly straight line for about two seconds before she parted them to down another slug of Scotch.

Harris raised his hands in surrender. "You're absolutely right, Ms. Barnes. You are entitled to an attorney. That is, if we are arresting you. I don't want to have to do that, and I suspect you don't want that either. I just need a few—"

Cole blurted, "You killed Karren Janson because you thought she was Molly Jones-Heitkamp!" He lowered his voice. "Gerald Payne already told me."

Harris jerked his head toward Cole. "The hell you say! What else are you holding back?"

Cole said, "He didn't say he saw her do it, more like he heard a thud and guessed it was Judith clubbing Karren." He didn't want to say too much, but he didn't want Harris any madder at him, either.

While they were talking, Judith staggered to the cockatoo and stuck her finger in the cage. "Pretty Boy, they're talking mean to me. Tell 'em what you think. Whadda you think?"

The bird fluffed its feathers and squawked, "Sorry bastard. Sorry bastard."

"That's right, Pretty Boy. Pretty Boy knows. Mama didn't do anythin' naughty. She promised to stay out of the way.

We had a deal. It would make everyone so happy. Me, you, and Jack, too. He understands. Isn't that right, Pretty Boy? Jack knows I didn't hurt his precious. He knows. He's going to marry me. He promised he would, right after the election."

Cole looked at Harris and opened his mouth to speak. Harris raised his finger to his lips and shook his head, motioning for Cole to help him. He quietly crossed the room and put his arm around Judith's shoulders. Cole caught her other side just as she started sliding toward the floor. They guided her to the sofa, her legs about as much help as wet spaghetti. She didn't resist when Cole lifted them onto the sofa as Harris lowered her head.

Harris said, "Now what's this about Payne? Isn't he the actor that taught Janice Phillips, aka Karren Janson, how to look like Molly?"

Cole nodded. "He may have been lying to get me to leave him alone. Maybe you ought to check it out."

"I'll do that as soon as I decide what to do with her."

She was starting to come around, groggy, head lolling, eyelids fluttering. She moaned. Lieutenant Harris patted her shoulder. She opened both eyes and looked as if she was trying to focus, then shook her head violently.

After several seconds, she zeroed in on Cole. "Why aren't you in jail? You should be in jail for killing that woman."

Cole squatted down in front of her. "I didn't kill her. Did you?"

Her smile wasn't intended to be friendly. "No, no, of course not. But . . . but they found her in your room. Your bedroom." She sat up and shook her head erratically. "They should've arrested your ass."

Cole's voice deepened with seriousness. "Who wanted me arrested?"

Judith's eyelids fluttered; she groaned and passed out again. Cole felt as helpless as he had when Linda said she was leaving. He looked at Harris. "What now?"

Harris shrugged and flapped his jowls. "I'll get some uniforms over here to watch her till we see which way the wind blows. If what you said about Molly's press conference is true, she may shake more than one tree." He pointed at Cole. "In the meantime, you stay out of it."

Cole's voice was loud enough to wake the dead, but it didn't disturb Judith. "Stay out of it! If I hadn't stayed in the middle of it, you'd have never found the drunk bitch."

Harris got red in the face, a crimson, angry red. The muscle in his temple twitched. "January, we don't need you. Don't you get it? We broke this case without your help. What do you think I'm doing here?"

Cole whacked his palm against the side of his head. "How stupid of me. I never dreamed you would show up here if Henrietta hadn't called you." He shook his finger at Harris. "That's it, isn't it? Henrietta called, but you were coming here anyway? Don't give me that shit. You couldn't find pussy in a whorehouse."

Harris said, "I'll have your ass yet, January. You still haven't explained why the body was delivered to you."

▽

21

WHEN COLE PULLED into the back parking lot of his office building, Rose turned in behind him. He had first tried to snake through the side streets to lose her, but decided it not only didn't matter if Rose followed him, it made sense for him to have a member of HPD to corroborate what he did next. With Fraizer watching Judith, Harris had decided Rose needed to keep up with Cole.

Cole smiled at Rose as she walked toward him. She'd never be accused of being underweight, but on her the padding looked good. Maybe this weekend he and Leslie could take her out for that dinner he promised. Kevin always liked Rose.

He held the office door open for her. "I've gotta make a quick phone call."

Rose stopped in the doorway and glared at him. "You could've called from where you were, January. There was no need to go sneaking back here, bouncing me over all the potholes in Houston. Harris said I had to follow you, he didn't say I had to tear the oil pan off my car."

Cole flipped the light switch. "What say you chill out, and we'll get out of here quicker than Judith slops down the sauce."

In the middle of Henrietta's desk, in red ink, was a note that read, "KEVIN'S COMING! FLT 204 FRIDAY 7:30 A.M."

Cole snatched the note from the desk. He looked down at it. Shook his head. Then wadded it into a tight ball and slammed it into the trash can. "She did it to me again!"

Rose put her hand on his shoulder. "How 'bout if you chill out, friend."

"Just shut up and let me think." The harshness of his voice surprised him. It wasn't that he didn't want Kevin to come. No, not that at all. But on Saturday, after he had this body-in-the-bedroom mess figured out. After he had time to shift gears—buy groceries.

Rose folded her arms. "That's enough thinking. There's lots of hours between now and then. You said you got stuff to do. Do it! And don't ever tell me to shut up again."

"Sorry," he mumbled. Cole knew she was right, but he wished that just once Linda would stick to the original plan. She always changed plans at the last minute. Sometimes, when he had other projects on his mind, he forgot to expect it. That's when it threw him the hardest.

Like the time they planned a quiet, candlelit dinner while Kevin was visiting her parents in Dallas. When Cole got home, the house was full of people. Linda had decided a backyard barbecue would be fun. It was, for her, but he hadn't been in a party mood. When it was over, she had complained that he wasn't romantic. He knew if he called and complained about the change in Kevin's arrival, she'd say he wasn't a good father.

He grimaced at Rose while he dialed. "You're right, Rose, I'll calm down."

Leslie sounded wide awake when she answered. Cole said, "What did you find out about Jimmy?"

"He checked himself back in. Isn't that great? The floor nurse said he's signed up for aftercare, too."

Cole wondered how Jimmy was going to take it when he found out Hoss had been murdered. At least he was in a place where he could get some help handling it. "Sounds like you're feeling better."

"I am. Anything else I can do to help?"

"Not right now. I'll be there as soon as I can."

When he hung up, he realized he could have told her about Judith. He decided he'd rather tell her in person. He turned to Rose. "If you're gonna hang on my tail, want to ride in my new buggy?"

Rose said, "It's about time you showed some sense. Let's take mine. The city buys the gas."

Cole didn't know what he'd say when he got there, but he knew where he was going. Everything was coming together. As soon as he added one more noodle of truth, he'd serve up the stew to Harris and get on with his life. After this, he wouldn't mind going back to serving citations and skip-tracing paperhangers. There was always work for a PI that could find a hot-check writer.

Tanglewild was one of the better neighborhoods, despite its age. The older homes were among the best when new. Some were updated, and some still had that fifties look—solid, but no distinguishing style other than big. Alissa's address numbers were prominent on the garage door. Cole could tell the arches and red tile roof had been added to the original structure to give the house a Spanish look.

Alissa answered the door. "Molly changed her mind. She doesn't want to talk to anyone, Cole. I'm sure you understand."

Rose took over. She flashed her badge. "She'll talk to us, or she won't be talking to anyone."

Cole pushed his way into the house. "I'm *going* to talk to her before she talks to the cameras."

Alissa smiled seductively. "My, my. Molly never said you could be so forceful."

"You're gonna see force in a minute if you don't tell me where she is." He charged through the den with Rose right behind him.

Rose pointed off to the left. "There!"

Molly was in one of the plushly padded wicker chairs in the sunroom, which had also been added to the original house. The large louvered windows, Mexican tile floor, and tropical plants made the room look larger than it was. It all worked together to make Molly look as if she were posing for *Architectural Digest.*

Alissa dashed around Cole. "I'm sorry, Molly. I tried to stop them."

Molly set the glass of iced tea on the glass-topped table beside her. "Never mind, but thanks. I'll talk to them."

Cole stepped down from the den threshold. "It's a good thing, too. First, I want you to know the killer has been arrested." It was almost the truth.

He sat down in the chair on the other side of the glass table. "Tell me again why Judith Barnes was on the list?"

"Because! She wants to marry Daddy, and she thinks I'm what's keeping them apart. Did she do it?"

"And you're not keeping them apart?"

"No! I don't care who he marries. Did Judith Barnes kill my stand-in?"

"If you don't care if she marries Jack, why did you give me her name? You must have thought she was capable of killing?"

"Well, yes . . . no. You're confusing me."

Rose was inspecting a hanging basket of Creeping Charlie and didn't look up when she spoke. "Either you thought she could, or you thought she couldn't. Which is it?"

"I don't know!"

Cole clapped his hands, faking enthusiasm, and leaned toward her. "Hurray for the truth. Isn't that it? You really don't know. Everything you've told me has been twisted and convoluted. You've lied, Ms. Molly Jones-Heitkamp. You've lied more than once. Maybe you don't know the truth about anything. I don't think Momma would have approved of that."

He walked away, then spun around and faced her. "Didn't you call Judith and tell her you'd make a deal with her if she'd meet you at the theater? She could have Daddy Jack if you could have the trust fund. You had already killed Karren—maybe accidentally—but somehow you set up Judith." He paused to drive home his logical conclusion. "To get her out of your way!"

He waited, hoping she would blurt out a truth in defending herself. When she didn't, he wavered. It all sounded plausible in his head. Logic be damned. There was nothing to do but charge ahead. "You don't get the megabucks when you turn thirty, do you? It all fits. You killed Karren. You had the leverage to make Hoss and Payne clean up the mess and ship her out in Jimmy's stereo box. Payne was desperate for the grant; Hoss was just as desperate to stay out of prison."

Cole nodded slowly. The longer he talked, the more he hoped it sounded like the truth. Still, he couldn't explain why they used his bedroom for their morgue. "It all fits except one little piece. You had them stick her in my bedroom!" he shouted. "Why! Why me?!"

She laughed one of those hollow finishing-school laughs. He would have never guessed she could do it so well.

She folded her arms across her chest. "You'll never prove it, because it isn't true. You're talking like a crazy man."

"You know I'm not crazy. Even if I am, I've got a policewoman with me. She's going to arrest your rich-bitch ass."

Alissa stepped into the room. "Molly, what's all the shouting about? Is there anything wrong? Do you want—"

Rose said, "Butt out, bitch, or I'll take you in with her."

Alissa staggered back. "I'll be upstairs if you need me."

As she turned to go, Cole said, "She's going to need a lot more than you can provide. I suggest you call her attorney."

Molly's eyes widened. "You're not serious, Cole. The Channel 11 crew will be here any minute. You can't arrest me now."

Rose walked toward her, smiling. "No, ma'am, he can't arrest you now, but I can."

She wasn't as fast with the bracelets as Fraizer, but she was smooth. "You have the right to remain silent. You have the right to have an attorney present when you are questioned. If you can't afford an attorney, one will—"

The timing was as perfect as any cavalry charge. Just as Rose concluded, the TV crew rushed from the van to Alissa's front door. Cole let them in.

Without any forewarning, the reporter shoved the microphone toward him. "Just tell us your name and what part you play in this drama unfolding behind the city elections."

Cole slapped the mike away. Rose threatened to arrest the

crew for interfering with police work. Molly screeched, kicked Cole's shin, and threatened to remove the rest of his hair with an axe. The cameras rolled.

By the time Rose stuffed Molly into the backseat of the patrol car, Alissa's neighbors were collecting across the street. As far as Cole knew, Alissa never came back downstairs during the big event. He suspected she'd watch the local news at ten, probably for the first time.

As Rose drove away with full sirens, Molly leaned toward Cole. "Now what?"

Later, much later, Cole drove slowly past Leslie's house. From the street, he could see the windows of the torture chamber and the kitchen. There was still a light on in the kitchen. He turned around and pulled into the driveway, wondering if dropping by so late was taking her for granted. He knew he wanted to be with her. He wanted to talk about the case with her. He told himself it was because she knew the details.

It surprised him that he wanted to discuss it at all. With Linda, he'd had to keep everything to himself. She didn't want to know. With Leslie, he wanted to hear what she thought about everything. And maybe, depending on how she was feeling, he wanted to let her know how he had missed being with her—how he wanted her.

Leslie opened the door wearing a cotton T-shirt that came below her knees and had a teddy bear on it saying "Hug Me." She was carrying a mystery novel titled *Blood Marks*, by Bill Crider. She held it up to him. "Don't read this when you're alone. If we ever get a case like this, it's back to Cedarbrake for me."

Cole took the book from her and carefully marked her place with the jacket flap. With smooth choreography he tossed it into the nearest chair, kicked the door closed, and enfolded her in his arms. "Just let me hold you for a minute, then I'll give you the update."

He followed the teddy bear's request and hugged it and

her long enough for his body to start responding; long enough to know he didn't want to let go. Pushing her to arm's length, he said, "How do you feel? Any sniffing or sneezing left?"

Leslie shook her head. "Nothing. My head's empty." She smiled devilishly. "Why? Do you have something in mind?"

Cole hugged her again. "Do I have something in mind? I really do." He released her and stepped back. "But it'll have to wait. How fast can you get dressed?"

She scratched her head. "I don't think a man's ever asked me that, especially this late at night."

"I promise I'll never do it again, but there's something niggling at the corners of my brain. I thought maybe if we went to the office and dug through some old cases together, I might be able to pull it to the front and take a look at it."

It took her less than five minutes to change. Once they were in the car, Cole explained the progress up to Rose carting Molly away.

Leslie said, "I bet you're wrong. She's the one who hired you. Why would she hire you if she knew about the body in your bedroom?"

"That's what I thought. But then I got to studying everything she's done. The threat that came in the mail. I never saw an envelope. She could have done that herself. The bomb, too. Then there's Payne and Hoss. They couldn't afford to cross her. See, if she knew that Karren was Jon's sister, and she knew Payne had told Jon to hire me, then she could keep tabs on whether I was getting close."

Leslie shook her head. "It just doesn't make that much sense. Even when you throw in your guess about the trust fund."

It was almost midnight when they got to the office. Cole started pulling files and tossing them on the conference table. "It's something little. Some insignificant bit that makes the difference. It always is."

Leslie yawned and stretched her arms over her head. "Where do you want me to start?"

Cole knew where he wanted to start, and it wasn't with

the two files he handed her. "These are both missing-persons files. Just scan them and see if there's anything that clicks."

"Whatever you say, but nothing's niggling my brain. I probably won't know it if I find anything."

Cole flipped open another file, then stood up. "I'll get something to make notes on."

From Henrietta's desk, he grabbed a couple of scratch pads and pens. As he turned back to the conference room, he noticed the file on the computer table. He knew Henrietta often left unlabeled files there when she was collecting background information or when she was trying to figure out something that puzzled her. She said she didn't want a client to come in and recognize someone's name on one of her files. It might shatter their confidence in CJI's discretion.

Curious, he picked up the manila folder and flipped it open. On the top paper Henrietta had written, "Ask Cole if he knows about this." Cole turned the page and read rapidly. He slapped the folder closed. "Bingo!"

He jerked the page from the file and walked back to Leslie. "Look at this."

Leslie read it, then looked up at him and smiled. "Well, you said it would be something small. I can't think of anything smaller."

"It explains everything, and it was right under our noses from the beginning."

▽

22

COLE HELD THE phone away from his ear while it rang. He knew Fraizer hated babysitting a suspect. It made the bear a bit grouchy. When he quit growling, Cole said, "Guess who."

Fraizer mumbled something that included Mother Frog, then said, "Where are you this time?"

"At my office." He didn't give Fraizer time to respond. "The R in Judith R. Barnes is for Ross. Ring any bells?"

"No! And if you call me here again, I'll ring your bell!"

The receiver slammed in Cole's ear. He slowly hung up and counted. "One, two, three, four . . ."

Cole picked up the receiver before it finished the first ring. He held it an inch or two from his ear. Fraizer's voice was loud and gruff. "Hot damn, Mother Frog! Is this some big secret you exposed?"

Cole said, "Remember the kid that hanged himself eight or nine years ago? My first solo case. His name was Tim Ross. Don't you get it? That's why the body was in my room—to get even for Tim Ross hanging himself."

"You're really reaching, January. There's probably a couple of hundred Rosses in Houston. What makes you think they're kin?"

Leslie came over and put her head on his shoulder. Cole stroked her hair. "Fraizer, I've got something to take care of, and then I'm going back to Judith's. What say you stay there and keep this under wraps till I show up? Maybe you'll get back on the lieutenant's good-boy list."

Fraizer grunted. "What makes you think I won't wake her up and take her in?"

Cole sighed and rubbed Leslie's back. He didn't know how much longer he could concentrate on his conversation with Fraizer. He cleared his throat to buy time to remember Fraizer's last comment. "Uh, from the condition she was in when I saw her, she's not going anywhere, unless it's on a stretcher to join Jimmy at the Banana Hilton."

Fraizer said, "You win. I'll stall if Harris shows up. Don't leave me hanging."

"You got my word."

"Yeah, and I know what that's worth, Mother Frog."

Cole lowered the phone to the cradle and backed Leslie against the wall. "You're not getting away from me now."

Her voice was barely a whisper. "I've never tried to get away from you, Cole January."

Cole covered the whisper with his mouth. As they slowly slid to the floor, Cole wished the contractor had used better carpet.

When they pulled up in front of Judith's house, Cole could see Fraizer's silhouette in the window. They got out of the Silverado and tried to close the doors quietly, but they sounded unusually loud in the wee-hour quiet. Dogs across the neighborhood did their duty and sounded a cacophony of barks and growls. By the time Cole and Leslie reached the front door, Cole doubted if anyone within three blocks was still asleep.

He pushed the doorbell. They waited. Nothing stirred behind the door. Cole didn't see how Fraizer could not have heard them. Leslie rapped loudly. Still nothing.

Cole pounded his fist on the solid wood. "Fraizer! Open up!"

Fraizer jerked the door open. "She's getting up."

Judith stood up and took two steps toward them. She almost fell as she staggered back against the sofa. "Whad're you doin' here? Where's Jack?"

She still had on the gold dress, but she had abandoned the shoes. Her straight dark hair was tangled and pushed up on one side, the side with the pillow crease across her cheek.

Cole caught her and guided her back down onto the sofa. "I don't know where Jack is, but I'm sure he's just fine. So what say you tell me about your connection with Tim Ross."

Judith's face contorted, and a visible shudder passed through her. "Timmy, Timmy. My baby brother Timmy. You killed Timmy." She smothered her face in her hands, wailing long, loud sobs.

Cole and Leslie looked at each other. Cole shrugged. He may as well go for it. "You know I didn't kill your brother, but I know you killed Karren Janson. You're going to serve a lot of time for killing that young woman."

Leslie nodded toward Judith and whispered, "She's stopped crying. Maybe she can hear you now."

Cole took Judith's shoulders and lifted her from the sofa. "You were trying to frame me!"

Judith wrenched away from him. Her eyes glazed over. "I don't have to talk to anyone about this. I'm going to marry Jack Heitkamp. I'll be Mrs. Jack Heitkamp."

Cole let her go. She walked with exaggerated care to the birdcage. Her voice became an eerie monotone. She laid her head against the metal bars. "Oh, Pretty Boy, what are we gonna do?"

Fraizer said, "Ms. Barnes, did you kill Karren Janson last Wednesday night at the theater?"

Cole could see that Judith didn't know where she was now, much less last Wednesday. She slid to the floor, muttering, "Jack loves me. Jack's going to marry me."

Fraizer scratched his ear. "Guess it's too late to read her her rights."

Just then, Johnson showed up. "Did you know we picked up Payne?"

Fraizer said, "I bet he fell apart like Humpty Dumpty."

Rose said, "So far, he's admitted to running Cole off the road."

Cole said, "I couldn't believe that wuss ran me off the road! Even after I saw the side of his truck."

Rose grinned. "He claims he did it. Might make for some good headlines. I can see it now." She ran her hand across an imaginary newspaper. " 'Wuss Wrecks PI.' Or maybe the rags will pick it up. 'PI from Houston Meets Wuss from Hell.' "

Fraizer slowly doubled over like a mountain folding in half. It was a silent, bone-shaking laugh. While he was laughing, no one else spoke. They all stared at him. Cole wondered if Fraizer was having a heart attack or stroke. It didn't sound as if he was breathing.

Finally, breathless, tears sliding down his face, Fraizer sank back on the couch. "Stop, Rose! I can't stand it!"

Cole said, "Put a cork in it, Fraizer. What say you tell me what other tidbits you've uncovered."

Rose's grin spread. Cole didn't like the looks of it. "Come on," he said, "What else?"

Fraizer stammered between giggles. "He said he nominated you for Sexiest Straight Man."

Rose elbowed Fraizer. Leslie's eyes widened. Cole unnecessarily motioned for quiet.

Judith's eyes took on the quality of someone looking at a distant picture. "The woman was heavier than she looked. We had a hard time getting her in the box. But we fooled that dumb wrestler. He thought it was a stereo. He shouldn't have figured it out. I caught her in the dressing room at the theater. Hit her from behind when she wouldn't look at me, wouldn't talk to me. She promised we could work it out. Thought sure it was Molly. Doesn't matter."

Cole was fascinated. It was like watching a dying movie star in slow motion. No one moved. Cole didn't want anything to break the spell.

Judith glided to the bar and poured herself a glass of Scotch. She sipped it, then weaved her way back to the birdcage. She didn't look at anyone. She was in her own world.

Leslie sneezed.

Judith stared blankly toward them, then turned back to the cockatoo. "It was that Cole January made Tim kill himself. Now they'll get him for murder like they should have when Tim died, Pretty Boy. I know how you miss Timmy."

Fraizer pulled out his handcuffs, but Johnson shook her head. They got on each side of her and walked her toward the door. She never quit talking. "When Cole January got suspicious, I shot out my own window. Clever, don't you think, Pretty Boy?"

Cole and Leslie followed them to the car.

Judith looked up at Fraizer. "Everything is going to work out. We're going to win the election, you know. Jack understands. Jack loves me."

Cole wondered who she thought Fraizer was. He also wondered if Molly was following the plan.

When Johnson straightened up from helping Judith into the car, she stared at Cole for several seconds before she said anything. "We'll take it from here. There's no need for you to go downtown."

Cole shook her hand. "Thanks, Rose. I still owe you and Fraizer a dinner."

"And we'll collect. But not today."

Cole and Leslie arrived at Molly's just before dawn. Every light in the house was on. Lieutenant Harris's car was at the curb. As Cole reached for the doorbell, Jack Heitkamp shouted, "I didn't have anything to do with that murder! Listen to me!"

Cole turned the knob. The door was open. He and Leslie walked in.

Harris said, "Well, well, January, still butting in, I see."

With a thin-lipped, wide smile on his face, Cole scratched his head like Stan Laurel. "Let me see if I've got it right, Harris. Someone from somewhere called and told you to come over here and get this awful person off the street, and you just naturally jumped out of bed and trotted over here to do your duty. That about it?"

Heitkamp pointed at Cole. "What the hell is he doing here?"

Cole said, "And I could ask you the same question. This is Molly's house, not yours, old man. Where is your lovely daughter?"

"It's none of your business where Molly is."

Harris said, "That's enough, January. We're booking Jack Heitkamp for the murder of Karren Janson, and I'm sure he will be under investigation for a few other offenses against the city."

Cole motioned toward the telephone. "Maybe you better give Fraizer a call. He should still be in the car on his way to the station."

Cole watched Leslie slowly lay her head back on the sofa. Just before she closed her eyes, she smiled at him. Cole waited for Harris to get off the phone. Heitkamp paced and muttered to himself.

When Molly entered the room, all three of them looked at her. Cole said, "Are you okay?"

Molly nodded. "I wasn't sure that it would work. I didn't know if I could hold the act together or not." She turned to Heitkamp. "Mother was right. You can't be trusted when money's involved. I'm glad she didn't live to see you now."

Cole looked at Harris. "Could I speak to my client in private?"

Harris nodded. "No objection from me. Take her back to the kitchen. I'm waiting for a couple of uniforms."

Cole grinned. "Oh? Did little boys blue lose their way?"

Harris shook his jowls. "You're gonna get all that trouble you've been begging for."

Cole said, "Promises, promises."

He left Leslie on the sofa, half asleep, and followed Molly to the kitchen. The predawn light washed the kitchen in a pale-orange glow. She reached into her handbag and pulled out her checkbook. As she wrote, she said, "I believe you earned this."

Cole wasn't going to argue with her. He said, "I'm sorry about the rich-bitch line. This hasn't been easy for you. You must really hate him."

Molly looked up at him. "No more than ever. I'll see that he's bailed out. That he has a decent lawyer. Then I'll pray they put him away." She lowered her gaze. "Like they should have the first time he hit Mother."

The officers arrived and hustled Jack to their car. Harris leaned into the car. Cole couldn't hear what was said, but it didn't matter. The case was closed.

He looked at his watch. Still two hours till Kevin arrived. He and Leslie slipped out the front door, holding hands.

Leslie looked wide awake. "I still don't understand about the letter-threat."

Cole grinned at her. "I thought you figured it out. Judith sent them. In the one to Molly, when she said 'Get out of his life,' she meant Jack's. In the one to herself, it was like the bullet through the window. A decoy."

Cole held the car door open for her. "Anything else?"

She smiled up at him. "I guess you're going to tell me why you were so awful to Molly, aren't you?"

He took his time going around the car. As he buckled up, he started explaining. "When I called Molly, we arranged the scene for the cameras. You're not going to think any less of me if I tell the truth, will you?"

When she shook her head, he continued. "It was Molly's idea. I merely helped her carry it off with style. She knew if she made a big enough stink, Jack would surface and run to hide his records and get rid of the gun he used on Hoss. It worked."

Leslie leaned her head on his shoulder. "Oh, Cole, you're so good."

"I know. What say I buy you a bowl of chili at Benny's Burritos, then we go get Kevin?"

Leslie leaned forward and looked at him. "I don't mind the trip to the airport, but Benny's? Forget it! That chili takes the hide off a buffalo. I'll send my stand-in."

Cole chuckled and squeezed her around her shoulders. It would be a cold August in Houston before he considered anyone to stand in for Leslie.